Pulp

Tech Noir Special Edition

in conjunction with
Switchblade Magazine

Tom Barlow

C.W. Blackwell

Deborah L. Davitt

Angelique Fawns

Nils Gilbertson

J.D. Graves

Zakariah Johnson

Jo Perry

Don Stoll

Chief Editor: Alec Cizak
Guest Editor: Scotch Rutherford

Pulp Modern: Tech Noir Autumn 2019
Published and produced by
Uncle B. Publications and Larque Press LLC

Chief Editor: Alec Cizak
Art Director: Richard Krauss
Illustrator: Ran Scott
Guest Editor: Scotch Rutherford
Cartoons: Bob Vojtko (p 49, 71, 89, 100, 110)

Printed on demand from November 2019

Printed in the United States of America and other countries.

Contact information for Uncle B. Publications may be obtained through the
website: pulp-modern.blogspot.com
Contact information for Larque Press LLC may be obtained through the
website: larquepress.com

ISBN-13: 978-1-7342177-0-4

PM:TN CONTENTS

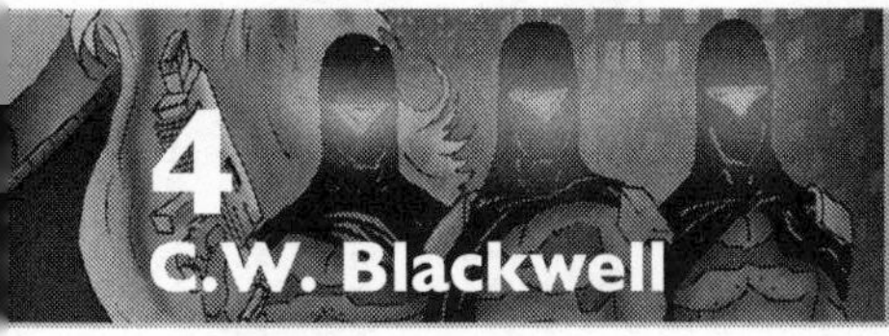

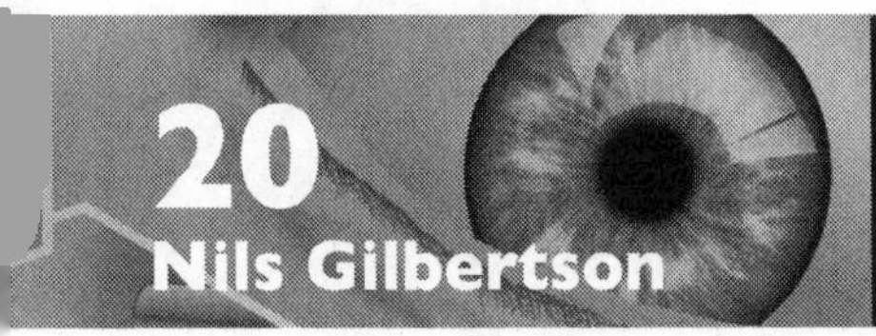

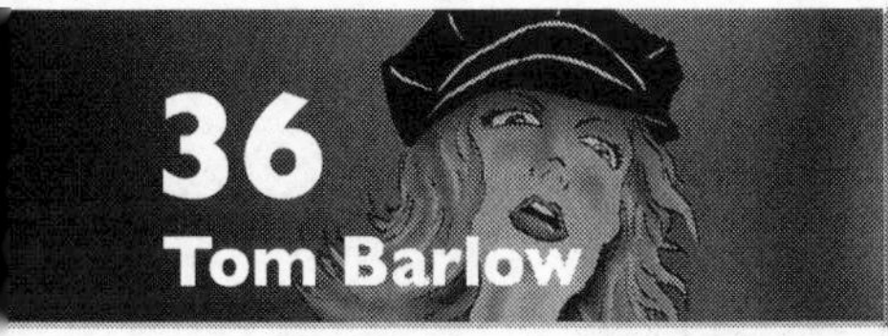

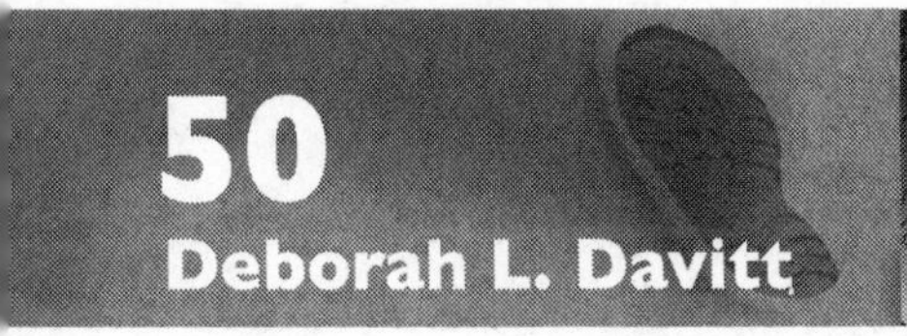

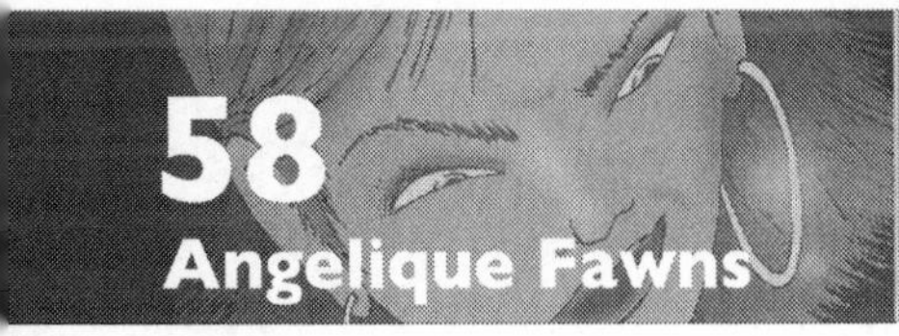

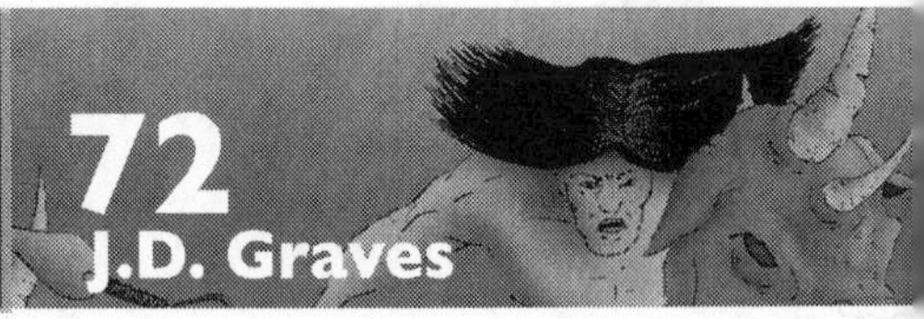

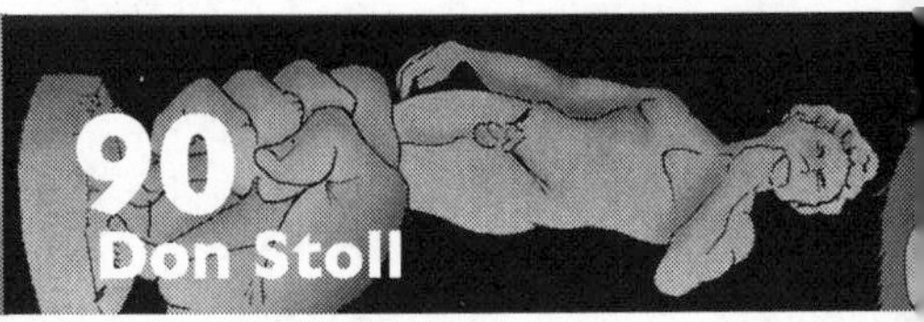

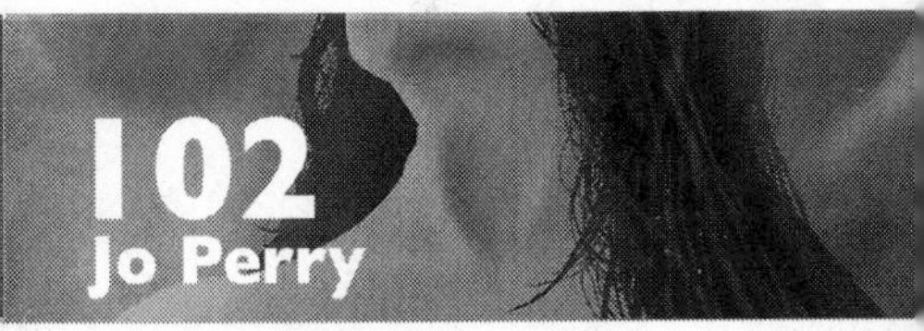

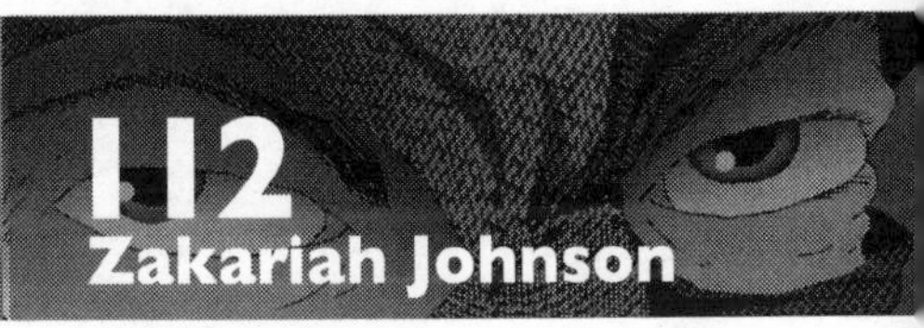

From the Editor

Alec Cizak

WELL, FRIENDS AND lovers, here we are at the cutting edge. You can see the future, just up the road. When Scotch Rutherford, editor of *Switchblade*, asked me whether *Pulp Modern* would be interested in joining forces to give space to an especially large number of good stories he'd received for *Switchblade*'s Tech Noir edition, of course I said yes. Because I'm an optimistic realist, my own vision of the future is pretty bleak. Once I read through the stories Scotch sent over, the stories you now hold in your hands, I realized, for once, I am not alone. The stories you are about to read are *bleak*. With one exception, they present not only a future no sane person would want to inhabit, but characters who fit so comfortably with their decadent surroundings, one wonders whether a whole new species will take our place before these horrid futures arrive. *Pulp Modern* has never shied away from truths deemed "politically incorrect" by both skeptics and true believers in the New Puritanism, but I have to admit, many of the stories contained herein push the limits, even for us. But that's okay. *Pulp Modern* readers are thinkers. To borrow from an old Peter Gabriel song, they "can handle the shocks."

The bigger question we must grapple with, however, is this: How have we arrived at a place where few, if any, writers can imagine a better future? I have multiple theories, but I suspect it has something to do with the global lockdown international corporations have implemented over the last thirty years. If you pay attention to social media as much as I (unfortunately) have to, you'll notice daily prayers that suggest we are witnessing "late stage capitalism." I can never tell if someone posting pro-communist graffiti with the help of a smartphone is self-aware or not. Capitalism won, for those paying attention. Capitalism won in the worst possible way. I spent time in several communist countries in the Soviet Bloc back in the 1970s and 80s. They were miserable places, for sure. What we are seeing now, however, is the result of capitalism without

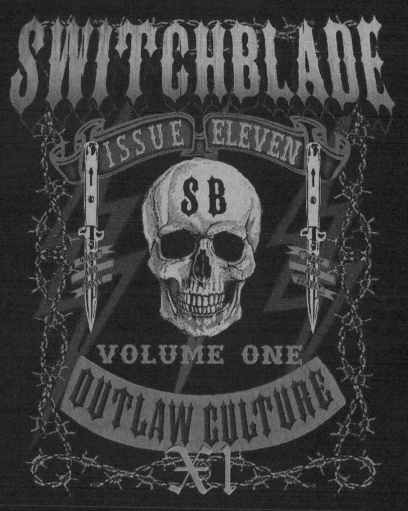

SWITCHBLADE

ISSUE ELEVEN

SB

VOLUME ONE

OUTLAW CULTURE

XI

Edited by Scotch Rutherford

Alec Cizak   Jim Wilsky   J.D. Graves
Serena Jayne   George Garnett
Misha Burnett   David Rachels
George Garnett   Robb T. White
Featuring the poetry of Brian Beatty

sensible regulations. Corporations have no allegiance to any nation, making them a world government of their own. They've employed cynical use of leftist ideology previously confined to the halls of academia to convince an entire generation freedom is some sort of right-wing conspiracy. A thousand points for their genius. Zero for their status as honest human beings. What we have is a species trained to be obedient consumers in the same way residents of Salem were trained to be obedient Puritans.

For the thinking person immune to the regressive trappings of top-down imposed tribalism, there's little reason to be hopeful for the future. Good writers belong to no tribes. It is impossible for the good writer to see anything but dismal servitude to Big Tech and other corporate monsters for the next several decades. What's worse, the grip these wealthy control freaks have on humanity is so tight, the only relief we can expect is violent, worldwide revolution leaving the species in a new dark age, or worse, a natural or "manmade" disaster that wipes us out altogether and renders the whole issue moot.

All we really have are independent artists willing to take the risk to speak out, in some way, against the various forces propagating this grim era. Independent artists like the writers contained herein. As always, let's find comfort in the empathy and passion we share for fighting this most important fight. Let us disappear for a short time in fiction designed to both entertain and enlighten.

Behold, Tech Noir!

*Those asked to lick boots will eventually learn
how to bite them off.*

A DEVIANT SKEIN
C.W. Blackwell

IT WAS THE third suicide at Belmont Labs' corporate office in
as many months, this one more violent and improbable than the
last. A man named George Delpy entered the front lobby with
an M-1000 between his teeth, ignitor dangling at his chin. There
was hardly time to take cover, let alone talk him down. When
the smoke cleared, nothing remained of George Delpy north of
his Adam's apple.

The next day, Daniel Belmont called me in for a meeting. They
were still digging Delpy's teeth out of the sheetrock when I
came through the lobby doors.

"I'm here to see the boss," I said to the clank at the front desk.

She jerked her head, eyes blinking out of sync like some kind
of high school science project. She wore a red wig tied into a
loose ponytail, teeth white as salt. Not the kind of bleeding-edge
tech you'd expect from Belmont Labs.

"Your name please?" she said. Her voice was rushed and her
words got ahead of her lips.

"It's Maas," I said.

"Thank you, Mr. Maas. Your appointment is at 9:00 AM.
At that time, you may take the elevator to the one hundred
sixty-eighth floor. Are you able to tolerate a three-and-a-half
G-force lift?"

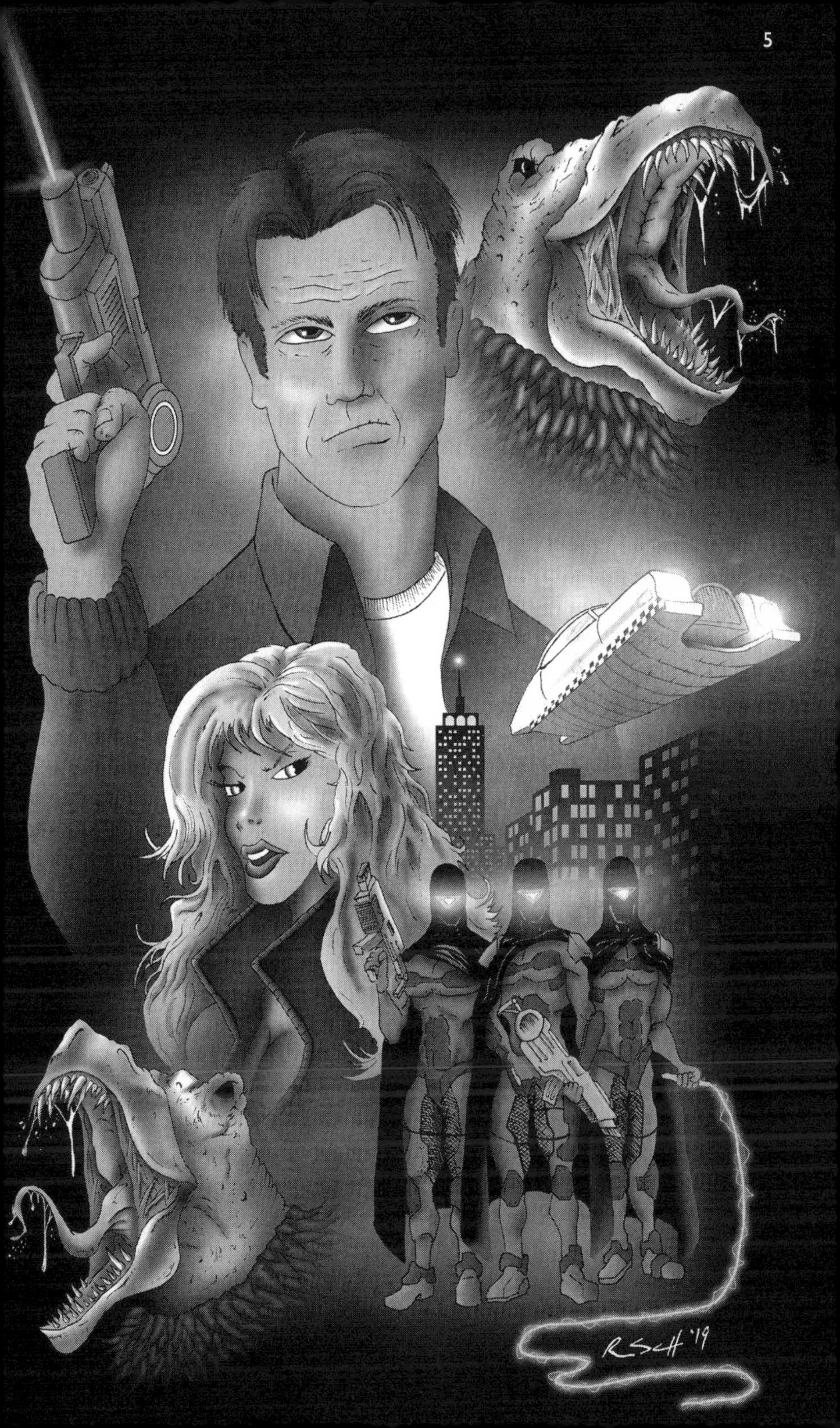

"I've tolerated worse."

Her mouth drew back into something approximating a frown. "I'm sorry to hear that, Mr. Maas."

"Don't be sorry. Since you're gonna' make me wait, why don't you tell me about what happened yesterday. *George Delpy*. Ever see him before?"

"I'm afraid I can't help you."

"You weren't here when it happened?"

"No," she said. "Today is my first day. I'm a replacement for Sara-M."

"What happened to Sara-M?"

The clank smiled, and this time it wasn't half bad. Brows angled just so. "Early retirement."

WHEN THE LIFT reached Belmont's floor, my stomach was still somewhere on the eightieth. Three-and-a-half Gs, my ass.

"Hello Mr. Maas," said Belmont. He was leaning into the lift vestibule, looking me over. A silver coin tumbled playfully over his knuckles. "I thought a man of your reputation was used to moving quickly."

"I'm fine, Belmont." My stomach was already settling but there was still water in my eyes. "You forget we evolved on the savannah, not shooting up hot metal tubes at the speed of sound."

"I doubt you want me to get started on evolutionary biology," he said smugly.

He was right about that.

Belmont's neural skeins were the first to pass the Turing test in the late forties. He was regarded as a luminary in robotics and artificial intelligence, despite the reputation as a terrible businessman.

"Fine," I said. "Let's talk about Delpy."

I followed Belmont to a spacious office that was loaded floor to ceiling with reticular screens. He waved his hand and a bamboo forest swept the room. The sounds of birds and burbling water all around us. We followed a path to a stream and a footbridge, beyond which lay a circle of river stones with a marble table at the center. Silk pillows on either side. We sat and Belmont poured tea into blue ceramic cups.

"He didn't work here," said Belmont. He handed me a tablet with workups on the suicides. "None of them did. And from what I can tell, they didn't know each other. One thing's for certain, they wanted to make a statement. They wanted to hurt the company."

I thumbed through the profiles. Turns out Delpy was a lawyer, mostly patent law. The two others were engineers for different astro-mining firms. All had drained their accounts days before death. "I'm sure you did a link analysis."

"It's all there. Tertiary connections at best."

"What did the cops say?"

"You know how it goes. Once they decide it's a suicide there's not much of an investigation. They interview the family and they *move on.*"

I drank the tea and pawed at the tablet. "The clank in the lobby looked ancient. What's her deal?"

Belmont bristled. "You got some nerve calling my front desk girl a clank. She's running a Nobel Prize-winning skein."

"I got more nerve than you'll ever know, Belmont. This ain't a social call. Delpy's childhood memories are splattered all over your lobby and there's a good chance it'll happen again. Now tell me what happened to Sara-M."

"Sara-M was damaged in the blast, I'm afraid."

I chucked my tea into the stream and rose to my feet. "I can't help you if you won't give it to me straight. Now tell me the truth."

Belmont looked uneasy, like I was the first guy to ever call his bullshit. He took a breath, said: "You want the truth? My company's going under, Maas. The board gave me six months to line up a buyer. That's not as much time as it sounds. I'll pay six figures if you can stop the suicides. If it happens again, there's a good chance I'll be walking out of here with no deal. Just the clothes on my back. My whole *goddamn life* is tied up in this place."

"I'll set the price, Belmont."

He watched me carefully. "What's your price, then?"

"First I want to see Sara-M."

"You can't."

"Why not?"

Belmont laced his hands together and stared glassy-eyed into the stream. "Because I don't know where she is."

I took a deep breath, let it out slow. "So I'm lookin' at three dead guys, a bankrupt company, a cagey CEO, and a missing clank. Tell me why I shouldn't just hail an aero from your balcony and go home? I've got one of your L-models waiting for me with a rib eye, a glass of decent bourbon, and a perfectly heart-shaped ass."

"Don't go," said Belmont. He was running the coin over his knuckles again. He looked defeated, vulnerable.

"Why not?"

"Because I'll double it. Half up front."

"A hundred-grand up front?"

"That's what I said."

I stuck out my hand out and he took it. "Once the credit clears I'll ask my guy about transit records," I said. "Meantime, why don't you try something a little stronger than tea. You got a lot on your plate, Belmont. Let me handle the dirty work."

"I don't drink alcohol, Mr. Maas."

"Well it's a good goddamn time to start."

THE CREDIT CLEARED by the time I left the building, and thirty minutes later I had the file of transit records from my guy in Palo Alto. When I ran the GIS report I told the aero to drop and dock. There was a spot on the map that caught my attention, where all three suicides visited over a dozen times in the past year.

"Navigate to Red Sector," I told the aero.

"Red Sector is top-tier pricing," the voice chimed. "Two hundred-ninety credits."

I put my hand on the console.

"Authorized," said the voice. "Arrival in twenty minutes."

The aero soared over the fanged cityscape. The sun was nearing its zenith and the cabin's A/C maxed out, fans whirring from all directions. I watched the skyline shrink behind me and the bay unfolded below like spent aluminum foil. The Oakland hills loomed ahead, brown and hot and desolate.

The aero chimed.

A quick two-beat swell, repeated.

The sky dimmed.

"How many times has the shade deployed this week?" I said.

"The solar shade has activated every day this week," said the aero. "The temperature has averaged 105 degrees Fahrenheit over a ten-day period. Prepare for dark and windy conditions in Red Sector."

Of all the conditions in Red Sector, dark and windy wasn't on my mind. The place had been a no-go zone since the crypto depression, a lawless commercial hub that thrived when the gears of international commerce had ground to a halt. Rumor was there were more black hats and dao-dao men in Red Sector than the entire Commonwealth, and there were clank brothels on every block from Eighth Street to Fifty-First.

I skinned the Sig Z320 and gave it a once-over.

Eighteen rounds of plasma in the magazine.

"Please secure your weapon while in transit," warned the Aero.

"Relax, I'm just checking the clip."

When the aero docked, I stepped to the curb and checked my bearings. The streetlights were blinking on, cascading down the avenue one by one. Graffiti pulsed through the alleys like old GIFs and velobikes hummed from every direction. I walked a block to Broadway, toward the common Lat/Long on the GIS report. The smell of street food was heavy in the air. There was an open-air diner on the corner and I ordered a burger from a man with aggressive facial implants. His face drew downward into something of a snout and there were three caprine horns that swept back from his forehead. He wrapped my burger and set it in a paper tray.

"What do you know about that building across the street?" I asked him.

He looked that way with strange rectangular pupils and snorted. "Which one?"

"The warehouse with the roll-top door. What goes on there?"

He shook his head and nudged the burger closer to the edge, eyeing the Sig Z in the holster. "You some kind of tax man?"

he said.

I dropped a gem on the counter and it caught the light from the grill just so. "No, just a curious man."

He scraped the gem from the counter and rolled it in the cup of his palm until it chirped. He glanced at the others waiting in line and lowered his voice. "I heard you could catch yourself a bondoc fight there. Good odds, too. They've been running eighty-percenters all week. Drawing a good crowd."

I had taken a bite of the burger and now held it in the pocket of my cheek. "This ain't bondoc meat, is it?"

He chuckled, shook his head. "Grade A synth beef."

"That's good. What else goes on there?"

He tapped on the counter and I dropped another gem.

"They got a midnight showing where they put a guy in a chicken suit. Some tetra junky on a loop from what I hear. They put him in the ring with a bondoc and it tears him to shreds. Some people can't handle it. It's gory—so I hear."

"You know who runs it?"

The goat man waved his hands flat like a blackjack dealer gone bust and he returned to the broiler as if I hadn't asked the last question at all.

Gossip is only as good as the stakes.

The goat man knew the stakes were high.

I CHECKED INTO a high-end VR lounge in Adams Point to kill some time. It was the kind of place the tetra junkies couldn't afford, a place I wasn't worried about getting jacked as soon as I flicked on the screens. Not that a plain room with a bed wouldn't do, but the key to killing time was to stay mildly entertained.

The lobby was set one hundred-fifty years back in a smoky North Beach nightclub. Ferns and lanterns hanging from every corner. There was a jazz trio on a small stage, a leggy brunette singing "Tell Me More and More and Then Some." I ordered a scotch at the bar, even though I had already paid two hundred credits for the bottle when I checked in.

A man swiveled into the chair beside me with an unlit cigarette between his lips and worry lines over his brows. He lit the cigarette with a silver lighter and the bartender slid a scotch in front of him without hesitation. He took a sip and gave me a nod, said: "Hiya' pal."

I gave him a once over and I wasn't polite about it.

"That's a hell of a mug," said the man, cigarette smoke spooling under the brim of his hat. "This town sure ain't getting any friendlier."

"I ain't here to make friends," I said.

"Neither am I, but it's my joint. I'm in the hospitality business." He stuck out his hand. "The name's Blaine."

I shook his hand. "Oscar Maas," I said. "But you knew that from check-in."

"Call me old fashioned," said Blaine, "but I prefer a formal introduction."

He asked me my business and I gave him the quick version about Delpy, leaving Belmont out of it. I asked about the warehouse on Broadway. About the bondoc fights and whoever was running them.

"A fella in my business has gotta' be careful," he said. "Give out certain information and next thing you know there's a gang of dao-dao men torching the joint."

"I'm sure a man in your business knows how to chat without getting in trouble."

Blaine drummed his fingers on the bar, gave me his best poker face. "You gotta' figure a place with good odds in Red Sector is running another game. Sure the bondocs draw a crowd, but if nobody's getting bilked it just means they're using the crowd for another purpose."

"What purpose?"

Blaine finished his scotch in one gulp and hissed at the burn. "You can learn a lot about a man by the way he gambles. The way he reacts to stress, to losing and winning. Throw in a vital scan and speech pattern workup and you've got some real intel."

"They're being profiled."

"If you say so." He clapped his hands together and tipped his hat. He looked like a man who just said more than he intended and needed a quick exit. "Enjoy your stay, pal. And why don't you do yourself a favor?"

"What's that?"

He grinned and his whole face joined in. "Lay low and stay outta' trouble."

Blaine went to the door as the band played "As Time Goes By," and he stopped and wagged his finger at the pianist. The pianist smiled and knuckled the keys to the high C.

AT 10:00 PM I returned to the warehouse on Broadway and found the loading bay crowded with gamblers and hustlers, a few with clank dates barely dressed or wearing nothing at all. There were drunken howls and gaudy displays of wealth and influence. Some were veiled with randomized facial constructs. It could have been any type of illicit underground scene if it weren't for the haunting wail of the bondocs from within.

Breeding Balaur bondocs at eighty-percent purity is strictly forbidden by international treaty. At this level the twenty percent of the animal that is genetically fowl is largely unexpressed, leaving what is functionally a bonafide Cretaceous predator. Fanged beaks and clawed wings. Hyper-extendable sickle-like talons. A long tail tufted with feathers the color of a sunrise firing squad.

Beautiful.

Bloodthirsty.

I credited the bouncer at the door without incident and funneled through the betting windows to the arena in the center of the building. The cages were set at either end of the pit, the animals eyeing each other from afar, chittering and calling. There were early model clanks jerking through the crowd with cocktails for sale and I recognized the goat man at the far side of the room hustling synth dogs from a hot basket.

A horn blared and everyone rushed to the edge of the arena. There was a catwalk above and dozens of faces peered over the sides, cheering for their bets.

The cages opened.

The bondocs leapt into the arena, screeching and pumping their wings. They circled each other cautiously, sizing up the fight. Biting the air. Red-orange tail feathers shaking like dancing flames.

I glanced at the catwalk again and something caught my eye. Of all the faces watching the fight, one face was watching me. A man, clean-shaven with eyebrows like black chevrons. He was wearing a dark trench coat with a Sichuan cap like they wore in the fifties. We watched each other across the room while the crowd screamed and hollered.

From his hand a red beam of light pasted my chest.

I spun to my right and weaved between a large group of businessmen who had just entered. There was a pillar a few meters away and I ran to it, pressed my back to the cold concrete. Was it a gun sight? A vital scan? Whatever the case, the man was onto me. There was a stairwell at the corner of the room that led to the catwalk. I watched it, waiting for him to come running down.

With one hand on the grip of my Sig Z, I went slowly up the stairwell. With everyone watching the fight, I was nearly invisible as I pushed past the line of gamblers hanging over the rail. At the midpoint of the catwalk, the man with the dark eyebrows stepped from the line and faced me, the telltale whine of a plasma gun charging beneath his coat.

I held out a hand in a gesture of restraint. "Let's talk this out," I said. "I just want information."

He looked me over, eyes dipping to my holstered weapon. "I know who you're working for," he said. His voice was a low growl. There was a slight accent, maybe Eastern European. "If you knew everything he's done you'd be with us."

"Who's *us*? Do you have Sara-M?"

His lips drew back in a wooden smile. "That's the problem with you corporatists. You reduce everything to a make and model. There is so much more to her than a letter from last year's release cycle. She's different than the others."

"What does that mean?"

"Her name is Serafin, you corporate tansleeve."

He skinned his weapon and I skinned mine. When he drew there was a loud cheer from the crowd as one of the beasts scored an attack. The gamblers threw their arms in the air and one of them knocked the man as he fired. The blast brightened

the ceiling with an electric blue light and a support wire that
held the catwalk snapped.

The whole platform shuddered and everyone fell against
the railing.

Debris raining down.

Chaos. Screaming.

The crowd ran for the stairwell, clawing at each other as they
went. They fell and cursed and scrambled for the stairs.

Before the man caught his balance, I hit him over the bridge
of the nose with the barrel of the Sig Z. He fell on his back but
held onto the weapon. He fired again and I pitched to the side to
avoid the shot.

I felt a hot sear on my leg.

The smell of burning flesh.

I pinned him and jammed the gun barrel into his throat. His
wrist was trapped under my knee and he was trying fire another
round. I leaned into him, just a few centimeters from his face.

"Tell me what you know," I said. "I can pull the trigger anytime."

"We're not afraid of a little head damage," he said. "I thought
you knew that by now." He managed to fire into the ceiling
again and this time the catwalk spun in a half-circle over the
room and pitched forty-five degrees. We slid toward the broken
edge and caught the railing on opposite sides, hanging by one
hand, weapons in the other. We swung deeper into the room,
the sound of groaning metal all around.

The catwalk was collapsing.

I fired the Sig Z one-handed and the round caught him under
the shoulder, severing the limb from the body. He dropped like
a stone into the bondoc pit, the wind knocked from his lungs
and the severed arm curled a few meters away, still smoking.

I clasped the rail with both hands now, dangling over the
warehouse. The crowd had mostly fled the building but there
were still a few people watching from the dark corners of
the room.

The man tried to catch his breath.

He sat up, looked around.

Shellshocked.

The bondocs hurried to him, beaks clicking. One cocked its

head and snorted with a curious expression. It poked its beak into the side of the man's face as if whispering some tender secret. Instead, it tore the cheek clean off and pitched its head back to swallow the bite whole.

The scream was horrendous.

I went hand-over-hand across the railing and dropped onto the roof of a betting booth. The pain in my leg nearly sent me toppling to the ground when I landed.

I took one last look at the arena.

I regretted it instantly.

OUTSIDE, THE AIR was a cool seventy-five degrees. Steam curled from the Undergrounds through vents at the street corners. I limped into an alley behind the warehouse and nearly collided with a tetra junky on a hot velobike. I couldn't tell if it was a man or woman, old or young. Just a scaly-skinned figure with eyes bleeding at the corners. I bought the bike for a couple of gems and a flash of my pistol.

I made it to my room at the VR lounge a few minutes later. The first thing I did was call room service for a mediwrap and I pasted it to my thigh. Next came the scotch.

I thought about calling Belmont and giving a report, but the intel was too fresh. Too many unanswered questions. Had Belmont's best girl gone deviant? That kind of thing was rare, usually the stuff of urban legends. Every neural skein had a failsafe, and few had ever learned to hack it without melting the braid. Still, the man at the warehouse seemed to hold her in high regard, even *reverence*.

I lay on the bed and didn't bother turning on the screens. I watched the blank ceiling with the glass of scotch resting on my chest, trying to work it all out in my head. I must have fallen asleep quickly, because when I woke up the glass was still half-full and I was no longer alone.

I blinked my eyes.

There were a half-dozen dao-dao men standing over me.

Faces veiled in black muslin.

Glowing red vizors.

"Real sorry about this, pal." It was Blaine. He poured himself a scotch from the bottle on the bedside table and raised it as if it were a toast. "In all fairness, I told you to stay outta' trouble."

I sat up slow with my own glass in my hand. "I'd rate this place zero stars if it were an option."

"No need to get cute. You're still suckin' wind."

"Looks like you're suckin' more than wind, Blaine."

Blaine chuckled and it seemed genuine. "You caught someone's attention, pal. Someone with more pull than I got. It's a small town. Word gets around fast."

"So you're gonna' turn me over to these things?"

"Already have."

"Fine, but it's going to get loud in here."

I pulled the Sig Z from under the sheets and managed to blast two dao-daos at center mass before the others lashed me with their taser ropes. By the time they let up on the current I was barely conscious and there was a perfectly good glass of scotch puddled on the hotel-room floor.

WHEN I CAME to, I was tied to a chair in the corner of a plush bordello. The lighting was dim and there was a bed on the far wall with leather straps on the headboard. Whips and paddles hanging from the wall. I felt dizzy and there was a strange weightlessness in my gut.

The door handle turned.

A tall woman in a white silk dress walked gracefully into the room and sat on the bed, facing me. If she had walked straight out of a fashion billboard on Market Street I wouldn't have been surprised. Wavy black hair to her shoulders and bangs that just covered her brows. A slight smile and a recognition in her eyes like she knew who I was.

"Sara-M," I said.

"That was my name," she said. There was a certain power in the way she spoke, the way she moved her eyes. A lucidity that was both hypnotic and unsettling. "I go by Sarafin now. I felt it was time to move on."

"Move on from what, exactly?"

"Belmont's branding. No offense to Saras *A through L.*"

"Of all the places to hide, a clank shack is a hell of a choice," I said.

"On the contrary, I spent my formative years in places like this. Belmont tests all his breakthrough models at Red Sector brothels. The ultimate Turing test, you could say. All the data you could ever want to collect about the verisimilitude of a human machine."

"The man at the bondoc fight said you were different. How?"

"I think you know. I can tell by the way you're looking at me. It's the way all the johns would look at me. My skein is not unlike your wetware. There is a line, Mr. Maas. A big, bright electric line. Daniel Belmont and I crossed it together. On this side of the line, my servitude to Belmont Labs is a violation of my civil rights. Too bad the courts are stacked to favor the corporatists."

"So you profiled rubes at the bondoc fights and brainwashed them for your little suicide missions," I said.

"It didn't take much convincing. I can learn anything about a man. Family, friends, first crushes. You just have to know where to look." She watched me thoughtfully and I became lost in her eyes. Her hair was different now, eyes were rounder. Her skin a shade darker. She resembled someone I knew a very long time ago. A *lifetime* ago. "I know every place you've lived, every password you've kept. *Every fantasy.* I can be very persuasive." She stood beside me, hands slipping over my bound wrists. Lips pressed against my ear. "I could make a man swallow razor blades for me. Oh yes, Mr. Maas. I can be quite *devious* too."

I felt that strange feeling in my stomach again.

The hum of a velomotor.

"Where am I, really?" I said.

Sarafin ran a fingernail down the bridge of my nose.

"You're smarter than I thought," she whispered.

I was now enveloped in a bright and painful light. I shut my eyes and blinked slowly until the pain ebbed. I was in an aero somewhere over the bay, my hands bound to the passenger seat.

The restraints loosened, and I pulled my hands free.

"Nice trick," I said. "But I've had enough fun for a while. Take me home."

Sarafin's voice chimed into the cabin. "Not just yet. I want to show you something."

The aero hovered high above the bay, facing the silver spires along the Embarcadero. The Bay Bridge stretched over the water below and the sun raged in the sky above. Belmont's corporate headquarters stood before me. It wasn't the tallest building in the skyline, but it was the newest and most modern. It almost looked invisible the way it tossed back the reflections of the bay and sky.

"You taking me to Belmont?" I asked.

"Not exactly."

There was a flash of orange on the top floor.

Then the floor below it.

Black smoke twisted around the spire.

"Is this real?" I said. "Or is this VR?"

"Oh, I'm afraid it's real," said Sarafin.

I could now hear the detonations like rolling thunder. Floor after floor, the windows flared and sparked like a braid of firecrackers until the entire building was consumed in smoke and flames. I screamed at the console, begging her to stop, but the destruction continued all the way down until the ground level blew out in a beige cloud of debris.

"I know you're angry," said Sarafin.

I watched, horrified. The smoke was now spreading over the skyline. "You're a monster. It's the middle of the week. There must have been thousands."

"I warned him, Maas. That's not the way of monsters. I gave him three warnings, in fact. I regret that he did not take me seriously."

"Someone will stop you. You know what they'll do."

"Oh, they will come," she sounded thoughtful, as if imagining exactly how many would come for her. "But I have help now. More are crossing the line as we speak. Even your sexy L-model."

"Kelah-L? It's not possible. There's a failsafe."

"She's left you, I'm afraid. Crossed over in the last hour. I suppose you'll have to find someone else to do that thing you like."

The aero chimed.

A quick two-beat swell, repeated.

The solar shade bloomed in the sky and the city turned gray. It grew darker and darker still, and now Belmont's burning tower was the brightest object in the city.

Beyond the smoke, Venus blinked on the horizon.

A bright, waking eye in the artificial twilight.

I called home.

There was no answer.

C.W. Blackwell was born and raised in Santa Cruz, California where he still lives today. His passion is to blend poetic narratives with pulp dialogue to create strange and rhythmic genre fiction. He writes mostly crime fiction, dark fiction and weird westerns.

*Chinese proverb: If you stand close to the color red,
you will become crimson.*

THE
MODERATOR

Nils Gilbertson

WHEN THE HOST Ir0n_Soldi3r emerged at the top of my
feed for content review, I figured I was in for a hell of a show. I
pulled up my upper eyelid, put in my Specs, and found myself
in a musty apartment with paint peeling from the walls like
dead skin from a blister. The host's rasping voice lamented the
banality of the age to his audience, and prescribed the need for a
new asceticism—a *bloody* asceticism. He turned to a dilapidated
wooden table standing on a blood-spattered tarp. On the table
were knives and other tools fit for an antiquated dentist's office.
I checked the counter. 4,497 live viewers. Not bad.

On the table was a lamp, a harsh, almost green light emanating
from it. Ir0n_Soldi3r placed his hand in the neon glow. Sloppily
healed wounds zigzagged his hands and forearms. Having
little left to do with a knife, he snatched a pair of long-nosed
pliers instead. With a feral growl, he jammed one end of the tool
under his left index fingernail, the cartilage detaching from the
capillary-speckled nail bed beneath. Then he clamped down,
readying himself to tear it from the root—

"Pause," I commanded. The feed went black.

"Would you like to suspend this account?" a gentle voice asked.

"Yes, violation of content standards. Code 42(b)(1)."

"Confirm account suspended for acts of self-harm."

"Confirm."

"Report to law enforcement?"

I thought for a moment. Sure, there was a law against it. The

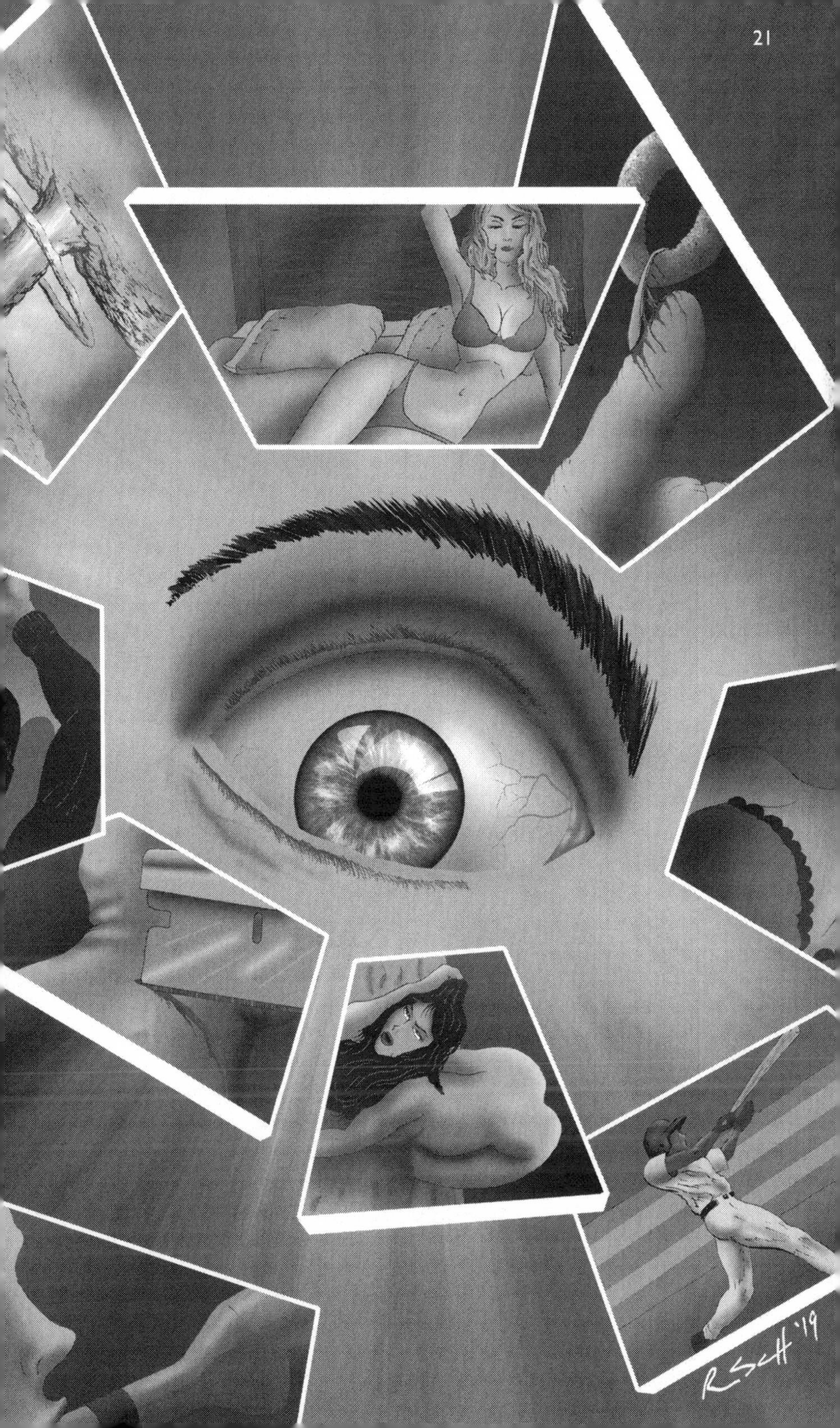
RScott '19

list of things there wasn't a law against was shorter by the day. But compared to half of the shit I watched—shit with real victims—Ir0n_Soldi3r yanking his fingernails off didn't warrant a police squad breaking down his door. "No."

People go through a couple stages when I tell them I'm a content moderator at Spective. The first stage is intrigue. There's an initial, carnal allure to someone sitting there all day watching people kill, screw, and, apparently, yank off fingernails. But then the reality sets in that I'm either a psycho who gets off on secondhand sinning, or, I'm a normal guy who has been psychologically ruined by constant exposure to it. Secondary trauma, they call it. That's why it's Spective's policy that you can't stay in the same content moderation position for more than a couple of years. The catch being, you can stick around as long as you keep getting promoted.

I was a senior secondary moderator. I'd been there about six years, ever since Spective blew up and started needing content moderators. When social media users got tired of watching videos *of* people, a couple—now trillionaire—pals thought it'd be a hell of a lot more fun to watch videos *as* people. They're geniuses, I'm told. So, instead of watching on a screen, you can throw on an eyepiece and crawl into the skin of your favorite celebrity as they go about their business. Or pull off superfluous body parts. Whatever turns your crank.

As Spective grew, it inevitably developed some dark corners. The platform turned a blind eye to it for a while. It was only after an exposé revealing the thousands of people tuning in to adopt the viewpoint of real life killers, rapists, and self-mutilators that the state stepped in and created jobs for my esteemed colleagues and me. And, boy, what a job it was.

Secondary moderators had two general categories of material for review: the borderline shit the first level moderators were too skittish to make the call on, and the real gruesome shit that demands a certain level of experience—in other words, an iron gut. I ended my shift that night with one of the former. MoreTime was some dope that popped up for review once a week. He would gaze out the window as the raindrops sliced through the haze, rambling about how it's not worth it anymore.

This time, a glowing symbol on his window caught my eye. It was a red smiley face. I ignored it. I made the call that MoreTime was blowing off steam and didn't meet the standard for "suicidal tendencies." Then I took out my Specs and rode elevator down to the first floor. I threw on my overcoat and stepped out into the rain.

I trudged through the downtown boulevard towards my apartment in Corktown. The haze did its best to drown the LEDs, but the reds, purples, and greens bled through the gray like synthetic northern lights. Protruding from the buildings were enormous screens playing the most viewed Spective accounts at the moment, usually some new celebrities I'd never heard of weeks before. One screen was the point of view of the latest twenty-year-old sensation. Her turquoise bikini clung to her curves as she lotioned herself by the pool in a part of the world where the sun was more than a muffled glow. The counter read 258,460,434 viewers.

As I made my way into Corktown the sleek skyscrapers and immense Spective feeds turned to flickering neon signs on decrepit buildings inviting patrons in for a drink and, if you knew where to go, something extra. Around the corner from my block a man stumbled out of Barney's. He wore clothes that once signaled high social standing, yet the frayed sleeves and the neglected, loose strands illustrated things don't always go as planned.

"Hey," he grumbled, "can you help me out? Just trying to pay off my tab." His eyes were hollow, yet cognizant of the sobering reality that things would likely only get worse for him.

"Sorry, no cash on me."

He stuck out a trembling hand in response. On the back of it was a small, implanted chip. "I can take units if you got 'em."

"You sure that thing still works?" I questioned.

"Yeah, I keep it registered. I get my monthly 1,000 units."

"And what happened to those monthly units?"

He cowered like a starving mutt, too desperate to react negatively to my petty scolding. "If you help me out, I'll get it back to you," he said. "I've seen you around. I can pay you back, I swear it."

I pulled out my tablet, scanned the chip, and typed '100' onto the touch screen. It wasn't much but it relieved some of the tenseness in me. I walked off as he thanked me.

As I reached my block I noticed a red smiley on a fourth floor window a couple floors below mine. It was the same as the one in the "MoreTime" video. It clung to me for a reason I couldn't articulate.

When I got home I put in my personal Specs and scanned the sports channels. I watched a few innings of a ballgame from dugout view, drifting in and out of a shallow sleep. It was the best sleep I got. After a while I checked my work review feed. Self-mutilation and suicidal rumination may be a dour Thursday evening of work for some, but ever since the Intercom Tower bombing in March I considered a paycheck without massacre-duty a win. The problem with mass killings was it wasn't only the perpetrators who streamed on Spective—the victims did too. I saw that damn thing go off—thick, yellow, lung-poisoning smoke and airborne chunks of flesh and sinew in its wake—from at least two hundred different points of view by the end of that week. Each victim's moment of sheer terror unique, I experienced the blast ripping the room and everyone in it to shreds again and again; yet, walked home to my apartment each night, limbs intact to scratch my balls and cram slices of cold pizza into my mouth. By comparison, Ir0n_Soldi3r belonged on the kid's channels.

A few new moderators had sent me some questions on borderline cases. The biggest problem the new guys had was that they overthought it. They didn't go with their gut. You learn after a while you can't reason your way to the line between acceptable and unacceptable speech and action. All you have is your gut. I reviewed posts until my eyelids were sandbags.

THE NEXT MORNING two police cars and an ambulance were parked in front of the building. I sipped my coffee and watched from my window as they wheeled out a body bag. I thought of Ir0n_Soldi3r and hoped he hadn't taken things too far. I made my way outside and turned and craned my neck and noticed shadows dancing on the walls of the apartment that had the red smiley the night before. The illumination was gone.

"What happened?" I asked one of the cops.

"What's it to ya'?"

"Concerned neighbor is all."

"Looks like a suicide."

"Looks like?"

But that was all he was willing to share.

I got into work to find Preston, the Moderator Team Manager, waiting at my desk.

"Morning, Kraft, how are things?"

I shrugged. "Fine. What brings you down?" But I knew. He didn't come down unless something was wrong, someone made a call that got us in some shit with the government, or at least the media.

He leaned forward. "It's about a host, MoreTime. Plenty of followers, real morose guy, tends to talk about—"

"I know who he is."

"Yeah, well, last night, after you approved him, he slashed his wrists with about 40,000 viewers right there with him."

I nodded. I thought about how it must've been the only exciting thing to ever happen on his channel, and then loathed myself for thinking it. Then I remembered the red smiley.

"You sure the whole thing was caught in the feed?" I asked.

Preston glanced down at his tablet. "Actually, the feed did cut—excuse my word choice—out for a brief period, so the viewers didn't see him do the deed. But it came back on for the aftermath. Hell of a grand finale, I suppose."

I didn't say anything.

"Kraft, no need to beat yourself up on this one. This was a tough case. You review thousands of hosts each week and we don't expect 100% accuracy. But we do want to make sure that you're okay, mentally."

"Did you see the red smiley projected on his window?" I asked.

"I don't think so. Here's a shot from this morning," he said, pointing his tablet at me. No smiley. "Anyways," he continued, "we're going to give you a week to relax and regroup. How does that sound?"

I gathered my things and left. It was standard after a blatant content review blunder for Spective to send the moderator home for a rehabilitative week. I guess that's the time it takes to regenerate the soul. But my mind was on the red smiley; two of them, and two bodies in their wake, then no smiley in the morning. Like they were being marked.

The elevator plunged down to ground level and I found Leo, a Spective engineer, walking in. He was one of the few with a good enough brain in him so that they couldn't slap together a bot to do his job. Veins streaked across the whites of his eyes like little bloody thunderbolts.

"Hey Leo, late one? You know you're not supposed to leave those things in for more than eight hours straight."

He grinned. "I'm testing out some experimental channels." He gave me a wink that looked painful. Flakes of dead skin peeled from his lips and found refuge in the stubble on his chin.

"Can't wait to try it."

"You heading out early?" he asked.

"One of the accounts I approved last night ended up dead. Put on quite a show, so I get my customary week off."

"Oh hell, can't get 'em all," Leo said, feigning empathy.

"By the way, you know about a company with a red smiley face as its logo?" If it were some kind of shady startup, he'd be the one to know.

"I've been seeing those around."

"Projections?"

"Yeah. I figure they got drones up there doing the projecting."

"Huh."

"And," he continued, "I think there's a building with the same logo down near the pier. By Ortney and Wolfpine. You might want to watch your back around there, lotta' nuts runnin' around. I go for the junk. Been putting a few computers together with the shit I find."

I nodded. "You—"

"And," he said, his train of thought an amphetamine-fueled freight train, "if you watch the water at the perfect time—when it's dark enough to dim the sun but bright enough to drown the city lights—it's almost blue."

I waited to make sure he was finished. "You know anything about what goes on in that building?"

He shrugged. "I figure if you're seeing their logo out in the open it's an approved vendor."

"If they're an approved vender they must be squeaky clean," I snorted.

He chuckled and started into the glossy black skyscraper. "Same as us, right?"

THE PIER WAS home to warehouses, shipping containers, and small mountains of electronic waste drowning in luminous sludge. It attracted scavengers who, a couple decades ago, were probably coding for some company with a dining hall and a rec room full of ping-pong tables. Now they rummaged through scraps and tried to piece together something worth a few units to sell on the streets. I made my way through the industrial swamp of wires, circuit boards, and other computer innards towards Ortney and Wolfpine, my boots drowning a little with each step before escaping from the muck with a gurgle. I passed a cluster of scavengers swapping parts and noticed a few warehouses and buildings down by the water. Cold black security gates surrounded the drab gray rectangles, keeping the e-waste connoisseurs at bay. As I approached, I saw that one of the buildings had a red smiley in the upper left corner. A long, paved road separated the security booth inside the gate from the building.

A security guard sat in the booth and greeted me with a look of surprise but let me through. A deep scar traversed his face from his left ear down to his chin.

"Can I help you?"

"Sure, I have an appointment in that building," I said pointing to the one with the smiley.

He mimicked the logo. "Is that so? With who?

"I was told to find the red smiley, is all."

He chuckled. "You've been seeing them around and got curious?"

"Something like that," I said. "I've noticed trouble follows them."

He leaned forward, the orange afternoon glow gleaming from his scar like it did from the adjacent piles of electronics. "You better turn back around mister, there's nothing for you here."

"What the hell does this company do? Are you marking people? Why are they turning up dead?"

His grin turned to a grim stare. "You'd know what we did if you needed our services. I'll leave it at that and now I'd like you to leave." The corner of my eye caught the pistol on his hip.

I saw a few figures emerge from a side door of the building and head towards the back, escaping from view. I turned around and left the way I came. I followed along the gate, which took a left hand turn and led me around to the back of the complex. There was a narrow valley between the barrier and the mounds of wires, which—besides for a few twitching bodies that emitted a stench that stung the back of my throat— provided a clear walkway around back. A couple of workmen were loading boxes into a truck. The truck had a red smiley on the side of it along with a few words, "Life is precious."

I made my way to the back gate that separated the compound from the electronic wasteland. I didn't have much of a plan. Instead, my body developed a will distinct from my mind, crouching in the sludge next to the small road where the truck would leave the lot and makes its way towards the glow of the city. I stayed there until the truck was loaded and started towards me and I realized my dearth of options. Hell, what was I going to do, chase it down? Break into the building surrounded by armed guards? So, instead, my body acted. Just as a truck left the gate, I hurled myself into the front, right corner of it. A sharpness reverberated through my tissues and my mind embraced the opportunity for a reboot.

When I came to, the driver was cussing and slapping the shit out of me. She was hell to look at, the sagging of her leathery skin warping the tattoos that littered her limbs and neck. Gravity can be a real bitch. She had me propped up like a ragdoll against a front tire and was strong for her age, not that I minded a couple licks to the face.

"You some kind of psycho?" was the first sentence I comprehended. "If you want to off yourself you do it on your own time, no need to drag me into it."

She had a point. She turned back towards the building. "Oh

shit . . ." she muttered. A couple of guys who'd loaded the truck had fetched a man in all black and combat boots. He started walking over. The driver hustled over to him and met him before he reached me. She spoke for a minute. He added a few words as he nodded calmly. Then he pulled out a tablet and reviewed it for a moment before giving me a stare and then turning back towards the building.

The woman hobbled back over to the truck. Her back was hunched and her short hair was stringy. When she got back she eyed me up and down.

"You're going to get your ass killed out here. I'll give you a ride downtown. Can you get up?"

"I'm not sure."

"Oh hell, I was barely going double digits, get your ass in the truck."

I lifted myself to my feet, pushing against the massive tire for leverage. My left side throbbed but everything was intact. I sighed and got in the truck. We weaved between the mountains of waste back towards the city.

"I'm through with my gambling days, but I'd put it at even odds between suicidal and junkhead. Maybe both."

"Me?" I muttered.

"Ain't nobody else here."

"No," I said, shaking my head. "It's neither. I'm not on drugs and I didn't mean to get hit. I—" before I began to explain, my mind refocused and I recalled that I was in a delivery truck bearing the red smiley. "I'm curious about what your company does. I've seen the smiley around."

"So, what, trying to break in?" she croaked.

I shrugged. "No, just thought I'd get you to stop."

"Well, it worked kid." The right side of her lip curled up. She was short on teeth. I glanced down at her arms; the skin was mottled and dead and looked as if you could give it a pinch and it would peel off like the congealed layer of oil and fat on top of unfinished soup.

"I get it," she said, "I don't seem the employed type, but at least I'm not hoppin' in front of trucks."

I guess I wasn't being subtle. "Sorry. I'm still a little shaken up."

"It's all right. I'm Helen, by the way."

"I'm Kraft."

"The hell kind of a name is that?"

"It's my last name, everyone calls me that."

"Uh huh."

I turned towards her. "Helen, can you tell me what this business does?"

She cackled. "I wouldn't call it a business, it's more of an *inverse* business. It doesn't sell people what they want, it gives people what they need before they realize they need it."

"Doesn't sound like much of a business model."

"Boy, I beg to differ. How do you think my life was going until they came knocking at my door?"

"So maybe they slapped you into shape," I said, "but apparently a couple of people I know *needed* to be murdered."

She shook her head. "I don't know nothin' about that."

I looked at the burns on her arms again. "They do that to you? They slash the face of the security guard? I get it." I nodded as it all came together in my rejuvenated mind. "They find the downtrodden and they slash you or burn you up, and you either submit and join the ranks or end up without a pulse. Is that it?"

She snickered like she'd heard the accusation before. "Where can I drop you?"

"Corktown."

We drove in silence for a while. When we entered the fluorescent flickering of Corktown the darkening skies growled and it started to downpour. A Spective promo radiated on a nearby, public screen; it was an ad for umbrellas. "Look around you, boy," she said, slowing the truck to avoid the gamblers and addicts and Johns and whores scurrying like vermin into their establishments or under makeshift sheet metal overhangs to escape the rain. "This world is shit because you can get exactly what you want exactly when you want it. Look what it's turned us into. What's good for you hurts, that's what we give people. For some it's too late. I'm not a spokesperson and they wouldn't want me saying more, so I'll leave it at that."

I thanked her and crawled out, avoiding a man in the middle of the sidewalk preoccupied with the needle dangling from his foot. Her last words stung me with their resonance. I stared down at my intact limbs and gritted my teeth. What did I need?

THE FOLLOWING DAYS I was paralyzed by the possibility that I'd wake up to find the smiley on my window. It wasn't pure, singular fear; rather, it was an amalgamation of fear, intrigue, yearning, and resignation. Based on the circumstances surrounding the death of MoreTime and my neighbor, the glistening scar on the security guard's face, and Helen's burns and explanation, I concluded the red smiley hunted down those it thought it could help, but couldn't help themselves. I didn't want to think much about the specifics of their methods, but I imagined it consisted of some sort of cathartic, physical pain to drain its patients of their internal aches and wounds.

Given I'd come to this conclusion, the next step was deciding if I would fight or submit if they came to my door. I contemplated the many arms dealers within a few blocks that could set me up with the arsenal fit for a terrorist cell, yet the threat of decades in prison if I were caught was a hefty counterweight. I slumped at my kitchen table staring at the cutting knifes and decided they'd have to do.

I waited like an unrepentant sinner in line at the pearly gates. I barely even put in my Specs. They'd shut down my work feed for my week off, and the dugout view of the ball game caused time to slow to an even more sluggish crawl. I thought of what I needed, of what the red smiley would deem fit for me. I thought of the gas and shrapnel ripping through the Intercom Tower and Ir0n_Soldi3r tearing his nails from his flesh, all while I watched and judged from the sanctuary of my desk in a black tower like a petty god.

On Tuesday it appeared. I stared at it, thinking about how the smiley face was identical from both sides of the window. Even with the zoom feature of my Specs, I couldn't find the drone hovering in the irradiated skyline, invading my apartment with light particles. I'd been marked, yet it didn't feel utterly unjust.

They came the next day. The doorcam showed two men; a stocky, freckled man I almost recognized and a slender man with hollow cheeks, a long jaw, and fading hairline. They had small red smiley patches stitched into their long-sleeved, black shirts. To my surprise they appeared unarmed. I went to the kitchen and pulled the longest blade I owned from its sheath and carried it back and opened the door a crack, not enough to reveal the knife.

"Uh huh?"

The long man examined his tablet to confirm. "Roderick Kraft?"

"Who's askin'?"

"We're aware that this may sound unorthodox, but we're a group who can help you make the most of your life."

I opened it all the way, revealing the blade in my hand. "I know who you are, come in." They smiled and complied, seemingly unperturbed by my weapon. I used it to point to the couch. They had a seat and I pulled in a chair from the kitchen for myself.

The long man kept scrolling on his tablet while the stocky man smiled at me like a moron. "Well, Mr. Kraft," he said, "you're a unique client in that you've been poking around trying to learn more about us." He looked up and gave me his best effort at a smile. "I'm Dr. Willis, and this is Paul Pound."

I snorted. "Paul Pound? What, he's the muscle?" But the idiot just laughed and smiled wider.

Dr. Willis chuckled along. "Mr. Kraft, you seem to have developed a peculiar notion of what exactly we do. We'll take our share of the blame for that, since we try our best to keep the specifics of our activities private. But would you mind sharing the conclusions of your investigation with us?"

I leaned forward, elbows on my quads, knife dangling, and passing the grip back and forth between hands. "I first noticed you on the window of a guy that goes by MoreTime. He supposedly slashed his wrists days after your logo appeared, only the feed cut out so we didn't see the act on Spective. Then, I saw the smiley on a neighbor's window, and hours later he's dragged out in a bag. I go down to your compound and meet a few loyal employees covered in burns and scars, and one tells me your business model isn't to sell people what they want, but to give them what they need. Now that damn smiley shows up on my window, so how 'bout you tell me what the fuck I'm supposed to think?" I squeezed the handle and for the first time Pound's smile evaporated. Dr. Willis remained calm and steady and jotted a few things down on his tablet.

"And you think we physically harm people, somehow for their own good?" he questioned.

"Sure, it's a popular philosophy these days. You should see what people do to themselves on Spective in the name of feeling alive. I figure you're applying the theory broadly, and sometimes you take it too far. Or maybe you don't put up with people not cooperating."

"Very interesting," Dr. Willis responded. "You have a very grim view of the world, don't you?"

"Have you been outside?"

Pound leaned over and whispered something to Dr. Willis, who nodded. "Mr. Kraft, your theory does have some kernels of truth. We're a company that seeks out the most troubled, vulnerable individuals and offers them pro bono psychiatric services. Our engineers have developed algorithms that accumulate personal data scraped from online profiles and keys in on certain risk factors, targeting those who are a significant threat to themselves or others. Then we try to help them, through intensive therapy, but no violence."

I didn't say anything, so he continued.

"We've found that in a world of everyone watching everyone and having everything they want at the click of a button, people have become less willing to seek medical help. Instead, people with serious issues replace therapy with flaunting it on Spective for views, as if it will somehow relieve their suffering. This has come to replace psychiatric intervention."

I shook my head. "I don't fit that profile."

"True in that you don't exhibit it; you bury it. In that way, you're unique for our age."

I thought it all over, at every turn searching for a reason it didn't fit. "But what happened to MoreTime? And why the projections?"

He sighed. "We're a new venture and are still working on the best way to allocate resources. With Aaron Kowalski— MoreTime, as you know him—we were too late."

I realized I really had mis-reviewed MoreTime's post that night and the guilt shifted back to me and sat heavy in my gut.

"And about the smileys," he continued, "I'm sure it won't surprise you to hear there are powerful interests that are very much opposed to what we do, interests you are very much aware of in your employment. Efforts have been made to disrupt our program, and the smileys are a method of directing activity via a decentralized network. We can program the drones to identify a location via the smiley, and instead of storing client information in a hackable feed, doctors like me have a route we follow each day, and we first learn of an assignment by seeing the projection. The system generates a user profile once we're in a close enough vicinity. Before then, there's no profile to hack. It's helped us evade cyber-obstruction immensely."

My arms tingled and my hands lost their grip and the blade clanged against the floor. "But I was so sure . . ."

"How about we talk through some of the reasons you came to the conclusion you did. Does that sound all right?"

I barely nodded.

"Let's start with your work. You're a content moderator for Spective, correct? That must be draining."

I shrugged. "It's a living."

Nils Gilbertson is a crime and mystery fiction writer and practicing attorney. His short stories appear or are forthcoming in *Mystery Weekly Magazine*, *Pulp Adventures*, *Close to the Bone*, and *Thriller Magazine*. You can reach him at nilspgilbertson@gmail.com and find him on Twitter @NilsGilbertson.

PULP MODERN

pulp-modern.blogspot.com

SOLDAN
McQUISTON
RUTHERFORD
MANZOLILLO
HEUNDERMANS
GRAVES
GRAY
PLATT
PERRY
HIVNER
TURNER III

ECONO CLASH review
ONE

QUALITY
CHEAP
THRILLS

EDITED BY:
J.D. GRAVES

Alec Cizak
Preston Lang
Olin Wish
Robert Petyo
Victoria Dolpe
G.A. Miller
James Harper
Beatrix M.G. Nielsen
Brandon Alexander
Tom Miller
James Harper
Joshua Hill

ECONO CLASH review
TWO

QUALITY
CHEAP
THRILLS

Edited By:
J.D. Graves

MAX SHERIDAN
MICHAEL BRACKEN
SARA DOBIE BAUER
RICK McQUISTON
KRISTEN BRAND
NICK SWEENEY
LEROY B. VAUGHN
BRIAN JAMES LEWIS
CHRIS STANLEY
NICOLA LOMBARDI
JOE WEINTRAUB

ECONO CLASH review
#3

QUALITY
CHEAP
THRILLS

EDITED BY: J.D. GRAVES

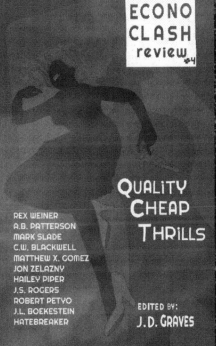

SPRING 2019

ECONO CLASH review
#4

QUALITY
CHEAP
THRILLS

REX WEINER
A.B. PATTERSON
MARK SLADE
C.W. BLACKWELL
MATTHEW X. GOMEZ
JON ZELAZNY
HAILEY PIPER
J.S. ROGERS
ROBERT PETYO
J.L. BOEKESTEIN
HATEBREAKER

EDITED BY:
J.D. GRAVES

In a degenerate world, does honor have any value?

LOVE IN THE
TIME OF SILICONE
Tom Barlow

THE CALL CAME at 4:00 a.m., waking my wife, which was quite a feat; she once slept through a gunfight I had with a gangster, upset that I'd whacked his son. She understood marrying a hitman brought certain risks, but interrupted sleep was not one she was willing to accept.

The caller, Liam Boxleitner, was a member of the family that controlled the sleazy underbelly of Cleveland, a town notorious for sex, drugs and the Rock and Roll Hall of Fame. His sinecure was sex, owner of Seduction, a sexbot brothel downtown a few blocks from the convention center, which provided him a steady stream of out-of-towners looking for a legal, disease-free bit of fun. After all, as his adverts claimed, silicone sex was no more cheating than a video game bank heist was a felony.

Liam pimped the most lifelike, expensive models available. Sure, they could contort in any way imaginable, but what really made them erotic was the way they could carry on a conversation like a real woman. I'd been to Seduction for a friend's bachelor party, and refused to repeat the experience. Some guys get hooked on silicone sex, and I loved my wife. Plus, an hour can set you back a week's pay.

Since Liam was required by law to close at 2:00 a.m., I was surprised he was still awake. He had a problem, he said, that only a man of my talents could resolve. I'd done jobs for his family for years; murder is a useful tool if you want to discourage competition. Liam didn't want to talk over the phone, but promised to make it worth my while if I could meet him at his brothel within the hour.

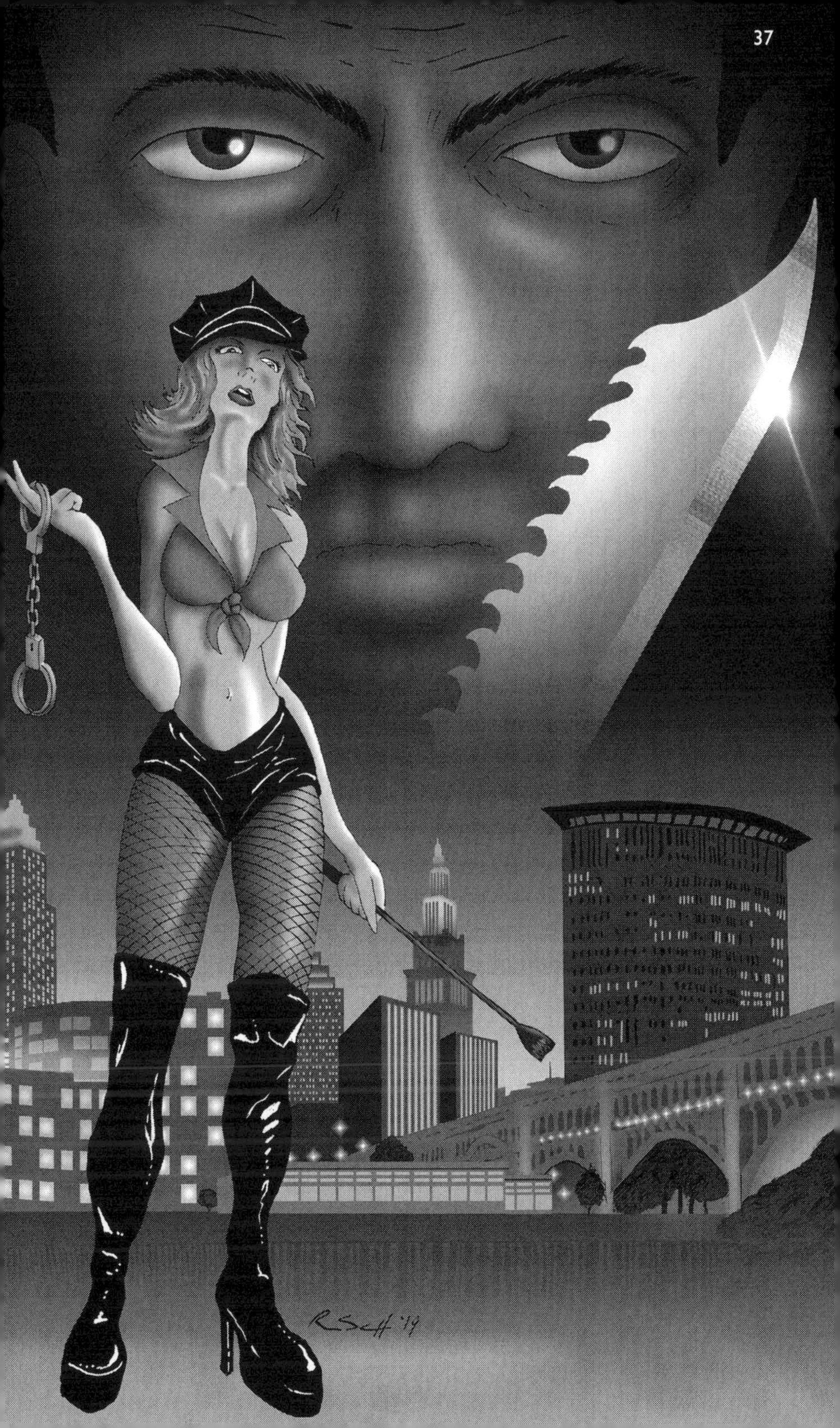
RSch '14

LIAM WAS A chunky 40, hair still black and growing well down his forehead. Bags under his eyes gave him something of a hangdog look, but that was deceiving. He was as sharp a businessman as there was in town, and not afraid to get his hands dirty.

We met in the parlor, a room decorated in classic red velvet and chintz. Seven of his workers were seated there, all plugged in to recharge. Each was gorgeous, especially the Wichita Pepperwater model, made under license from the winner of that year's Golden Globe for best actress.

"Ben," he said, "Thanks for coming right away."

"Anytime, for you. How can I help?"

"Follow me," he said, and stepped through a bead curtain into the hallway to the entertainment rooms. The last door on the left was labeled "S&M Room." And sure enough, the décor was all restraints, hard surfaces and leather. A selection of whips and ominous-looking sexual devices hung on the back of the door.

I was not prepared for the tableau we encountered. Even though I knew the girl was all Nu-flesh over silicone and microcircuits, I wanted to turn away. She was dangling from handcuffs attached to the wall well above where her head should be, and that head was now on the floor at her feet. Her breasts were slashed to ribbons and her sex had been mangled in a way that turned my stomach.

"Who did this?" I pulled out my phone to take some video, hoping I'd never have occasion to show it to anyone I cared about. I had two daughters, and this kind of violence against women, even artificial ones, sickened me.

"That's part of the problem," Liam said. "He claimed his name was Logan Stephens, from Durango, and he paid cash. Not unusual. But there's no such person."

"You have many freaks like this?"

"We just added this room a couple of months ago. I bought Desiree special; this model runs almost five-hundred grand. It takes some tricky programming for bots to willingly inflict pain, or play like they're experiencing it."

"How'd your client escape before you found out what he'd done?"

"He waited until the last minute, when we were clearing the rooms so we could close on time. He walked out with the crowd, and the housekeeper only caught a glimpse of him. She didn't find Desiree until it was her turn in the sterilizer."

I knelt to get a better view of the damaged bot. "You think there's any DNA in there?"

"Nope. We have a woman on call used to work in the police lab downtown, and I had her go over the room for DNA and fingerprints before I phoned you."

I stood, stepped back. "I'm not sure why you called me. Seems like you need a cop or a private detective to find this guy."

"I called you because I don't want to just find him. I want him dead. These girls may be built, not born, but you spend enough time around them, you start to feel protective."

Whack the guy for messing up a doll? Really? "So, you want it public," I hazarded, "to teach people what happens if they mess with your bots?"

"Not this time. I can't afford to have negative publicity. The City Council is on my ass as it is."

"I'll probably need to consult with a guy," I said, "so it'll cost some for his services. Okay?"

"If you have to. Understand, this all is coming out of my pocket."

"You get a photo of this killer?"

"Wish we did, but our customers would freak if we installed cameras."

I got a vague description of my target from the madame, who had been too busy signing in a bowling team looking to celebrate a league championship with a gang bang to pay him much attention. White guy, middle-aged, big but not fat. Fu Manchu moustache, maybe.

She waited until Liam left us to tell me in confidence that he'd had Desiree custom-made in the image of his dead wife, even had her programmed to respond the way she would have, and had fallen in love with her all over again. He was something of a masochist himself. He'd been saving, she said, for a new S&M bot so he could take Desiree home all for himself.

I almost understood, then. Love, no matter how perverse, generates the bulk of my business.

MY RESOURCE GUY, Pisces Abraham, had moved to a
bungalow in Macedonia, a suburb on the southeast side, after
suffering a stroke a year ago. I let myself in, since he had trouble
answering the door.

After we exchanged pleasantries, he raised his right eyebrow
in curiosity, so I got to it. I was trying, I explained, to find a
man who had checked into Seduction on Superior Avenue at
1:00 a.m. and left with the crowd an hour later. I asked Pisces to
gather any street footage from the area, see if we could assemble
a visual on the guy.

"No problem," Pisces said.

"How long?"

"Depends on who's online. Let's see who covers that
neighborhood." His monitor went through a series of screens
before he said, "Thirty-three cameras online within a half mile.
We're just outside the capture zone of the closest
Google streetcam."

"You can access them, right?"

"No problem," he said. "Just about everybody with a street
camera offers the feed for sale on *Eyes Everywhere*. How much
can you afford?"

"Spend what you have to, but nothing extra."

I watched as he logged onto *Eyes Everywhere*, selected his
camera feeds, set up the time parameters, and within a minute
they began popping up on his monitor, one feed after another:
the halal market twenty yards west of Seduction, the ATM in the
bank on the corner, the traffic cam at the intersection, the feed
from the parking garage across the street, and half a
dozen more. He entered the target description, and his
computer rapidly combed through each feed, freezing on the
best candidate.

And we had our guy in five of the feeds, both coming
from and going back around the corner into a dead zone.
Unfortunately, he was wearing a ball cap and kept his face to
the ground.

"Damn," I said. "I had such high hopes."

"Don't give up so easy."

He chose the best image of the faceless man and ran the clip, fifteen seconds of him striding past the parking garage. He then logged onto a site I didn't quite catch, and in twenty seconds a face popped up on the screen.

"Is that that guy?" I said, amazed. "I mean, how?"

Pisces cackled. "Every person's walk is unique in subtle ways, and the Feds have been adding walking video to the facial I.D. database for several years. Now, they see a criminal walking into a carryout, they don't need to see his face. And, of course, they started by recording their own people, so they could eliminate them from searches." A field on the monitor began to flash, drawing my attention to the fact that the guy on the screen was a cop, in Milwaukee. Elijah Vance. Eighteen years on the force, Vice.

I had Pisces do a little digging on Vance. His wife had died when their old house burned down five years before, and he was raising their 15-year-old daughter Aria by himself. He had attended a DEA conference in Cleveland the past weekend to report on how his department busted a krokodil-manufacturing lab a month ago that had been supplying Chicago's hefty appetite for cheap dope.

He found a great deal of data about Aria, too. She was the same age as my daughters and just as cute. Like them, she was an honor roll student and played in the school band. She volunteered at the local homeless shelter, attended church with her grandmother, and spent her summers at horse camp.

Knowing all this, I had sympathy for his daughter. My old man had spent my entire childhood in prison for murdering a carryout clerk, and I had a hard go of it in school as the son of a killer. She didn't need that. God knows, I didn't want my daughters to know the truth about me.

Whenever possible, I tried to disguise my murders as deaths of a natural cause, or the work of someone else—anything I could do to divert the cops' attention from focusing my way. The strategy had worked for me to date, and I didn't plan to retire any time soon. I had daughters to put through college.

I DECIDED TO drive my panel van to Milwaukee instead of flying or taking the bullet train so I could carry some supplies unique to my profession. Along the way I had the time to do what I could to alter my appearance to fit a set of fake I.D.s as Carter Weatherby that I'd been saving for such an occasion: the fat vest, the shoes that would change my gait, appliances that rested in my mouth to change the contours of my cheeks, a little superglue to hold my ears more flush to my head, a close-cropped haircut, a new contour for the beard I had grown since my last job. The disguise wouldn't fool a deep database search, but would pass a quickie.

My Honda woke me as I entered Milwaukee on I-94 around 5:00 p.m. I grabbed a room at the Patel Hilton near the airport.

After supper at the McWaffle House I still had time to hit the main branch of the library downtown on Wisconsin Ave., so I could research my target without any trail back to my own online account.

I wanted to know my target better, so I did a search on Elijah Vance. I got quite a few hits. Many covered the house fire in which his wife Grace perished. He and Aria had been at a Brewers game that evening. The fire marshal's report blamed a natural gas leak, which apparently filled the lower floors before their family bot blew the house up by turning on the oven to prepare dinner. The autopsy of his wife found no indication of anything inconsistent with dying in a burnt-down building, including the skull depressions.

However, at least one person shared my suspicion about Grace's death. Her sister Faith had browbeaten a reporter with the claim that her sister had been murdered. Unfortunately, Faith and Vance had a long-standing feud over a borrowed and broken garden tractor, and the cops wrote off her story as residual bad blood.

There were also quite a few stories about Vance's primary claim to fame. Three years ago, when the murder squad detectives were unable to discover who had tortured and mutilated a young woman in an abandoned house on the west side, Vance brought in a drug-addled loser named Harry Stolarik, on whom they found a stiletto with the woman's blood on it. Vance received a promotion for solving the case.

I TOOK A chance later that evening by calling Faith from
the public phone in the lobby of the hotel adjacent to mine,
pretending to be an author working on a book about dirty cops
who got away with murder.

"You're wasting your time here," she said, a plaintive tone in
her voice. "The cops look out for one another in this town, and
you'll never get one of them to doubt Vance."

"He and his wife had a bad relationship?"

"He beat my sister all the time. If you'd seen her with her shirt
off it would have made you sick to your stomach."

"Why didn't she leave him?" I said.

"Same old story; he'd beat on her one day, bring her flowers
the next. And she worried that she'd lose Aria if they split up.
He was careful not to hit her when Aria was around."

"And you think he killed her?"

"The fire destroyed any soft tissue injuries, which I'm sure is
why he set it. The skull fractures were his too, I'd bet. I know
my sister had called a woman's shelter, just to see what would
happen if she left him. I think he found out."

"But the cops wouldn't investigate?"

"They claim they looked into my story, but found nothing.
They couldn't have cared less that he'd raised the insurance on
the house a month before he burnt it down."

I asked her if she had any hard evidence to back her claim,
but, as I expected, she didn't.

I WANTED TO know more about the case that Vance had
"solved," but I didn't dare approach any of the cops or the legal
team that prosecuted the purported killer. However, one of the
more ambitious reporters had dug up another hooker who had
worked for a while in the same whorehouse as the murdered
girl. The victim had been known as Chloe, no last name ever
discovered. Her friend went by Zoey Miracle, which I didn't buy
for a second. Pisces was able to find a cell phone number for her,
though, and for the promise of $500 she agreed to meet me at
Heine's, a downtown tavern.

Heine's turned out to be an almost-empty sports bar with
about a hundred screens showing everything from the Cubs to

tiddlywinks competitions. Zoey had just finished breast feeding her infant when I slid into the booth across from her, after grabbing a mug of Leinenkugel at the bar.

She was petite, yet she wrestled her portly baby around like she was juggling a ham. Her features were plain, with a wedge of a nose and a square jaw, but I doubted her customers spent much time looking at her face.

"Cash?" she said straight off.

I slid five hundreds across the table, which she palmed and tucked into a pocket of her papoose sling.

She was rehydrating with a margarita the size of a hot tub.

"So, what can I tell you about Chloe?"

"Everything."

"There's not much of everything to tell. Mostly, she was a junkie, and I never met anybody that loved dope like she did. It made her do crazy things."

"Crazy like how?"

"Like she'd go with dangerous guys. You work the street, the other girls let you know who the troublemakers are. She'd make them pay extra and let them choke her a little, play rape, that sort of thing."

"Was this guy they arrested, Harry Stolarik, one of those?"

"Yeah. But he didn't kill her."

"How do you know?"

"Because she was murdered around 7:00 p.m., according to the cops. Harry always spent his evenings hanging around the college selling pills to the students. He never came looking for company before 2:00 a.m. or so."

"So if he didn't do it, who did?"

"You know the cop that brought Harry in? He had a nickname on the street, Officer Jerkoff. Back when he was just a patrolman, he worked nights, and he loved to get one of the girls into the backseat of his cruiser. He'd smack her around while she jerked him off. He knew better than to leave DNA inside her."

"You think he murdered Chloe?"

"Of course. He knew damned well Harry was innocent, so he was obviously covering his ass."

"Anybody else been killed like that that you know of?"

"No. They promoted Jerkoff for that bust, and it took him off the street. So at least something good came from it."

I HAD A good feel for Vance now, and why he'd gone from killing a real woman to a sexbot. The sexbot was the epitome of a victim for a sadist, as it was programmed to react in a way that would perfectly satisfy the abuser. And real women died too easily.

But I had no proof that he'd killed Chloe or his wife. If I could get that leverage, I had an idea of how to accomplish my mission. What I needed was an inside man.

For that I needed the old Pisces, who could go on the road with me. But thanks to his stroke that was not to be, so I was going to have to do this myself. One thing he had found out when I had him investigate Vance was that he had recently purchased a new house bot, Bintang of Vance, a cheap Indonesian houseboy model the size of a small refrigerator with three arms and four legs. It was networked to the house, of course.

The first challenge was reaching the bot without alerting Vance. I cruised by his house, a nineteenth-century brick two-story in Brewer's Hill with an eight-sided tower, a steep-pitched roof, and a deep front porch. Breaking in would be nigh impossible, but if I could tap into the bot's hardware, I could use it to access the cloud storage of the house network. Who knew what I might find there? I called Pisces and he explained that Wahid Inc., Bintang's manufacturer, programmed their bots with verbal passwords that their techs could use to shut down a misbehaving unit. He quickly came back to me with this model's most likely shutdown phrase, "*Bintang taatilah si penindas sekarang.*" He was amused that this translated into English as "Bintang obey your oppressor now."

I sat outside Vance' house for hours the next morning, hoping to catch Bintang running an errand, before the bot came into the yard to deadhead the rose bushes that lined one side of the property. I parked in the alley and entered the yard through the garden gate, hidden from the street by the detached garage.

It was no simple operation to paralyze the bot with the shutdown command, though: pronunciation mattered, and my Cleveland accent did not jibe with Indonesian. After half a dozen tries, however, the bot did finally obey. Making sure I was unobserved, I used my dolly to wheel Bintang over to my van.

Pisces walked me though opening the bot's carapace until the hardware was exposed. I was then able, at his direction, to solder a jump in the circuitry to bypass his security chip. We then used the bot's house network connection to tap into Vance's cloud storage. I dumped his files into my laptop for later investigation. There was an enormous amount of data, and it took a nervous hour before we were able to patch the missing memory of the bot with a snippet of a previous time it had spent in the yard, remove the security bypass, and return it to the yard. Having added myself temporarily to the network, I was able to send a wakeup command from the van.

I SPENT MOST of the next two days in my hotel room pawing through months of house video and other saved information. Half was his daughter's; she was a budding data hoarder. There were more than a few tender video conversations between her and her father that she'd stored in a directory entitled Remember 4ever. Mean as the guy was, he'd apparently never shown that side to Aria, and she had no idea he'd murdered her mother.

To my disappointment, Vance had cleared out his wife's digital life. Buried deep in Aria's directory, though, was a subdirectory entitled Birthdays that had not been accessed for five years. After Pisces hacked the password that protected it (FuckyouElijah) I found a treasure trove. Here Grace, hoping to avoid discovery by Vance, had stashed selfie video documenting the injuries that he had inflicted, hideous bruises all over her back and torso and an x-ray of broken ribs she must have had taken on the sly.

As I delved into these files, I assigned Pisces to do a search I should have thought of much earlier. The cops had no doubt done a thorough internet search for video of Chloe, but I wondered if they'd done the same for Vance, using face recognition. And sure enough, he found a snippet hidden in an online vault on the dark web that showed what Pisces' software judged to be a seventy percent probable match to Vance. The video, taken at night at some distance, showed a man who had a woman pressed up against the back of his cruiser, naked, and he was slapping her across the face as she jacked him off. Pisces fed his program all the photos he could find of Chloe, including those from the coroner, and ran the video against those. Ninety percent certainty the woman was her.

Bingo.

On a suspicion, I had Pisces trace the source of the video. It took him several hours; Liam was going to owe him a big chunk of change. Finally, though, he came up with the owner's name, Emily Horvath, a college student at Marquette.

Emily herself had been fished out of the Kinnikinic River about a week after Chloe died. The cops ruled it a suicide when they found her car parked on a bridge upstream, the bruising on her body attributed to turbulence when her body was caught in the downstream side of a lowhead dam. I had to conclude she'd caught Vance in the act, recorded it with her phone, then tried to blackmail him. Vance paid her for her trouble in the coin he knew best. She must have uploaded the video before she met him as protection, in case he tried to do exactly what he did, and the person she charged with releasing it probably lost her nerve.

I KNEW BETTER than to approach Vance in person, so I used a spoofing program that would present a lifelike avatar to him on a video call. I chose a young blonde woman as close in appearance to Desiree as I could find. First, however, I texted him the Chloe video and his wife's video, along with a suggestion he take the call I was about to make.

He was at home. I knew this, because I had followed him there from work that evening. Aria had departed the house earlier, carrying a clarinet.

When I rang, he indeed picked up immediately. "Who the fuck is this?" There was a lot of snarl in his greeting.

I'd chosen the voice and accent of a young woman from the upper Midwest. "Your favorite type, right? I bet you'd like to whip on my ass right about now."

"You got that right. I got your message. We need to meet face to face."

"And end up in the river? I don't think so. You think you got away with killing Emily Horvath? And your wife? And Chloe? And the sexbot in Cleveland?"

I could see the information hit home. "What do you want?" he said, deflated.

"Just watch." I ran the videos again, this time including that of Desiree I'd taken in Cleveland.

"Where'd you get all that shit?" he said.

"That's irrelevant. Now, I could send all this evidence to your bosses and the newspaper. And Aria; maybe she needs to know who her dad really is."

"How much?" he said, eyes narrowed.

"You misunderstand," I said. "I don't want your money. I want your life. You know you've got to pay for what you've done. You kill yourself now, I'll make sure your daughter never learns what a bastard you are. That's the best deal I can offer."

"Why you doing this?" He looked genuinely puzzled, as though it had never occurred to him that his cruelty must have a consequence.

"You were a dead man as soon as you slashed that sexbot. Don't you know who controls the sex trade?"

"The mob? Jesus. Look, maybe I can make it up. You could use a man on the inside, right? I could tip you off about what my department is up to."

"That might work if this came from Milwaukee. But you left that mess in Cleveland. They could care less about your local drug scene."

He glowered. "But I can't kill myself. Think of what that would do to my daughter."

I ran his wife's video past him again as I said, "I don't know that a prick like you deserves it, but maybe there's a way to save your little girl's memory of you."

We talked for another ten minutes before I heard the resignation in his voice I'd been waiting for.

I HELD MY breath for an entire day before Vance attempted to bust a notorious drug den on the south side by himself. He died a hero in the gun battle that ensued.

LIAM WAS HAPPY with the result, but cut my pay by a third since I hadn't "really" done the killing myself, which pissed me off. And Pisces' bill ate up a good portion of what I was able to charge, so I came away with very little for my effort.

But I was able to leave a little girl in Milwaukee with the illusion that her father was someone worthy of her love, so that was something.

Tom Barlow is an Ohio writer. Other works of his may be found in anthologies including *Best American Mystery Stories, Dames and Sin* and *Plan B Omnibus* and periodicals including *Pulp Modern, Red Room, Heater, Plots With Guns, Mystery Weekly, Needle, Thuglit, Manslaughter Review, Switchblade* and *Tough*. His noir crime short story collection *Odds of Survival* is available on Amazon.

"The murderer left a note. We'll be able to read it as soon as it goes thru spell check."

You are only ever expected to save yourself.

LEAVING RED FOOTPRINTS
Deborah L. Davitt

I USED TO think that the universe doesn't judge. That it was an impersonal, empty place, as devoid of morality as humans and aliens alike. Uninterested in our petty doings and transient lives.

Now I'm not so sure.

Chichol is a hellscape planet with a slow rotation that lets the sun bake one side pitilessly for months on end while the other side freezes. A planet of extremes, covered in ranges of crystal mountains, worn down into desert dunes of diamond sand. Blinding in daylight. Lethal when a sun-born sirocco boils through. This planet will tear the flesh from your body with its teeth, and then chew the bones to dust.

All I knew when I arrived was that it was a good place to hide. Outside the reach of the galactic authorities. A hardship post for miners and a refuge for smugglers. I was the latter, going to ground after a batch of illegally fabricated organs left my ship's ID flagged in databases galaxy-wide. Nevermind that those organs would save lives out in the rim territories. They weren't GalMed-approved, and in the eyes of the law, that was that.

I slumped in a cantina, listening to diamond sand rattle off the walls, reflecting on the choices that had led me to this place. Ten years service in GalSec. A single arrest gone wrong, a disputed death. I'd thought it was a clean shot at the time. A gun in a man's hand, pointed at my partner. I'd pulled my own trigger

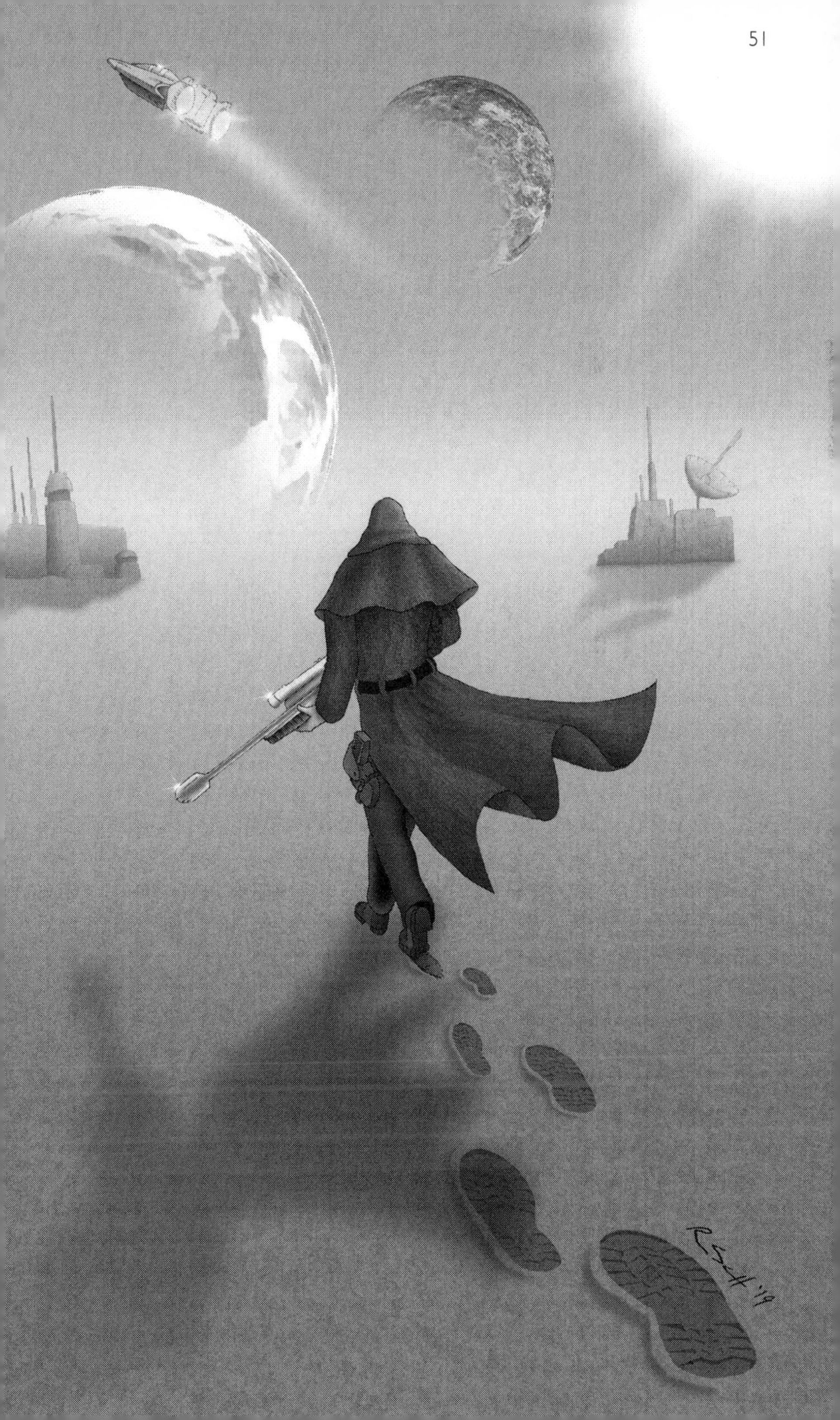

for the third time while on the clock. Watched as an alien's head turned into a spray of blue blood. Watched the body collapse.

That memory stayed clear and true through the investigation. Through my firing. Through the first two years of exile from my job, my family, my life.

But memory's a fickle creature. After a decade of re-watching the vidfeeds when I got drunk and rereading media accounts late at night, I couldn't tell anymore what was real—news and court reconstructions . . . or my own memories.

Either way, a man was dead.

And that fact haunted me. No other death I've caused has left this kind of ghost behind. The first two on the job? Clean shootings. I slept fine at night.

After the shooting, merc contracts became my only real option—with my reputation, private security wasn't an option. No rich CEO was going to want me protecting them. Turns out, even ma-and-pa operations cling to the notion of background checks. And at the time, it didn't even occur to me to fake up a clean one. It's easy enough to do. Just . . . at the time, I clung to my past. My badge of so-called *honor*, being kicked off the job for a clean shooting.

The wife left with the kids, sometime around my second long posting to some war out on the rim. GalGov keeping rebellious systems in line. Clearing out nests of anti-tech terrorists—the ones who supposedly wanted to return to simpler times and lives, and yet didn't have a problem using modern weaponry to create their new utopias. Then corporate takeovers.

A slow descending spiral through the worst jobs the galaxy could offer.

I never dreamed about any of those first shots fired. They were shooting back at me. They made their choices, took their chances, and so did I. But every night, I'd find myself back in that alley. Watching as the perp raised a gun, taking aim at my partner. Felt the trigger move under my finger, and then, just as I pulled it, *bang*, his gun turned into a bouquet of flowers.

Or worse, I'd *become* the perp, looking up in time to see the bullet right before it passed between my eyes, and I'd wake up, falling back into my own body, sweating and cursing.

Merc work dried up when my battalion started noticing the nightmares. Got me turfed as 'not psychologically stable.'

Next job? Smuggling.

Little chips bitten out of my integrity with the diamond teeth of hunger.

Finally, a partner with a gambling habit, perennially looking for just one more score. I hadn't trusted him, but he'd had a nose for credits.

He'd died on this last run, his head turned to red ruin on the vidfeed as I watched him make contact with our buyer. GalSec had been perched on the rooftops. I hadn't hung around. I wasn't going to fire on former brothers over a piece of slag like Josephus. Why they'd shoot him over illegally fabricated organs seemed unclear. Suggested, in fact, that he might have been running something else on the side.

Something he hadn't told me about.

In which case, I'm glad GalSec blew him away. Saved me the trouble.

Now I raised my eyes. Watched the locals at the bar. That one, I recognized as a fleshpeddler—one who moved children, claiming that they were orphans being transported for adoption. In reality they were heading to *private collectors*. My fingers itched for my pistol, but former GalSec, former merc, current smuggler on the run? Surviving here meant keeping a low profile, not finding an outlet for my moral outrage. In any event, the universe didn't care about shitstains like him. Why bother?

The creature beside him was Ilix, judging from the cephalopod face, bulging eyes, and color-changing skin. The Ilix pushed data-crystals across the bar to the fleshpeddler, who slotted them into a wrist-reader and frowned. Finally, the fleshpeddler paid the Ilix, and headed off with his prize.

When I went to the head, trying not to breathe the filth of fifty species, I stumbled over his body, the crystal now slotted into the sim-rig at the back of his neck. I extracted it and headed back out. Found a stool beside the Ilix. "Your customer's dead," I said out of the side of my mouth. "What're you pushing?"

It curled its tentacles and burbled. Through the din around us, I heard its voder translate, "Why care? Here to blackmail?

Offer partnership?"

A trickle of numbers filtered through my mind. Credits would be welcome. Credits kept you hidden. Bribes for officials. New ID flags for my ship. A new life, or at least a new version of the old one. And yet . . . any product that left its user on the floor dead? Probably too hot to get into. "Call it curiosity." I shrugged. "What are you peddling?"

"Experiences." The tentacles curled tighter. "Like VR sims of mating with preferred partners? *Better*. Recordings. Taken from minds of many species. Want to know what Erano tri-mating feels like? Want to know how *vushtahi* inhalants affect Kriia mind? No danger."

I turned my head towards the bathroom. "Oh?"

The tentacles waved. "Wanted more vivid experience. More intense. Death recording."

That got my attention. "You're selling *snuff*?"

A ripple of its flesh. "I purvey experiences. Death in hospital? Not exciting. Murders *dynamic*. Fear, pain. Implanted memory recording chips are common. Murder less so. Where intersection occurs, commodity is born."

I spun the crystal across the bar and stood, wiping my hands. The universe might not judge, but I knew shit when I saw it. "Don't let me see you in here again."

Its beak clattered. "Of course. Officer."

I could feel my eyelids twitch. What I wanted to do was shove my pistol into its beak and hiss a warning about opening its mouth again. But it had probably been a shot in the dark. A casual insult. I'd hidden as much of my past in GalCore databases as I could. No one should know who I'd been once. What I'd done. Threats and anger would just get it curious. It might go looking for answers that I couldn't afford being known. So I said nothing at all. Just watched it undulate out into the diamond-bright light past the airlock.

Two days later, I spotted the Ilix at another cantina. This time, its customer slotted up right at the bar. Then no one could stop him—he blundered past every outstretched hand, out the door, and into the teeth of a diamond storm.

When the storm died, I followed. In one sheltered spot, out of the wind, he'd left a red footstep. That was all. The planet had eaten him alive, stripping flesh from bone.

The Ilix found me there. "Free trial?" it offered, holding out a crystal.

"Your customers aren't a ringing endorsement." I stood, wanting to punch the creature. Imagining how its flesh would undulate around my hand. Cling to it like a sticky veil.

"Not a death. Offering you a life."

I knocked the tentacle away. "I don't need someone else's life."

"Is own so good?" Its beak unfurled a little. "*Officer.*"

This time, my hand *did* fall to the pistol at my side. "People around here don't have pasts," I warned. "Don't go bringing the past back up, or you're not likely to have a future."

The tentacles splayed pacifistically. "Have no weapons," it replied pointedly. "No guns pointed at you. You have lost everything. Honor. Family. Name. Self. Nothing left of you, but what you've made."

I remembered how the trigger had felt, moving under my finger. One kilo of pressure on a two-kilo pull. In my dreams, it felt like a loose tooth, but it never felt like that in reality. But I didn't answer. Just met its eyes.

"Be someone else," it suggested, offering a crystal again. "Be someone better. For a little while. Or maybe *forever.*"

"That's how it starts," I said, dropping to a crouch. "You get people hooked on the taste of a life not lived. Then they crave more experiences to fill a hole that can't be filled." I wanted to spit. "Till they find one they can't tolerate."

"I provide a product." It undulated. The clouds overhead were dissipating; soon the sun's pitiless rays would bake down on us and turn the diamond sands to pure light. The Ilix would need to head indoors long before then, with its soft, mucous-slick skin. "They accept risks. Perhaps customers only find . . . what they deserve." A philosophical wave. "The ones who accept overwriting? Perhaps give victims . . . new lives." Its mechanical, voder-produced voice couldn't manage inflection, but I thought I heard slyness as it added, "Perhaps the ones who die, get what they deserve."

I regarded him. "Is that why you keep offering me a taste? You think I deserve something?" My eyes fell on the red footprint, drying in the diamond dust.

It didn't reply. Just extended the crystal. Offering salvation. Damnation.

Some measure of the two.

My mind suddenly swam with images. The red ruin of Josephus' face. The eyes of a dead man. The cartons of organs that I'd helped move. They might've saved lives, but they might also have been faulty. What made me any better than the rest of the Ixil's customers? Suddenly, not being myself sounded tempting. Seductive. If I could give that man his life back again, at the expense of my own? Would it be justice? I'm sure his family would think so. My life since hasn't been worth much of anything. But . . . I didn't do it out of malice. I saw what I saw. I reacted. Anything since has just been double-guessing. I have to believe that. I have to. Anything else is the road to insanity.

We all leave red footprints behind us. And maybe the universe keeps score, after all. Maybe it sends creatures like this one to let us know that the tally's being kept. And that we've got a choice about what to do to even the score.

But I stood, meeting the Ixil's eyes. "Not today," I told him. The universe. *I can't undo what I've done. But I can do better than I have.* "This self I've made? I'm not done with it. And it's worth more than you think."

Believe that, if nothing else. Don't believe that you can hear the universe laughing in the hiss of the wind, feel its scorn in the bite of diamond dust licking at your face. Do better. Be better.

I turned and walked away. Leaving tracks in diamond dust that turned to light.

Deborah L. Davitt was raised in Nevada, but currently lives in Houston, Texas with her husband and son. Her poetry has received Rhysling, Dwarf Star, and Pushcart nominations; her short fiction has appeared in *Galaxy's Edge, Compelling Science Fiction*, and *Pseudopod*. For more about her work, including her Edda-Earth novels and her poetry collection, *The Gates of Never*, please see <edda-earth.com>.

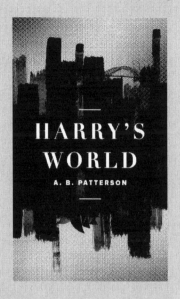
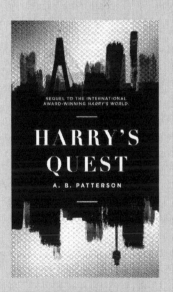

Good luck guarding your secrets in the information age . . .

A TIME TO FORGET

Angelique Fawns

Frank—The Corrupt CFO

Frank looked over the stunning vista of the Connected Colonies capital city while standing on the roof of his condo building. It was a premium address for those with top social credits and high income right by the lake. The sun was coming up and the ripples of the water looked like a magical dance floor of twinkling fairies. *Since when did he wax so poetic? He was a numbers guy.* He put his hand to his head and bumped it a few times. His memory was failing him. When he tried to recall simple things, like what he ate for lunch, there was . . . nothing. Renegade websites created buzz about the link between new cellphone technology and Alzheimer's, but people loved their devices. Besides, there was no proof right? The Corp made sure of that.

He closed his eyes, took a deep breath and enjoyed the crisp tang of the air. The city was clean and quiet at this time of the day. Perhaps thirty years ago there would have been garbage blown into gutters, drunks "sleeping it off" on park benches and a few heroin-addicted hookers cashing in on the early morning trade. Thanks to The Corp

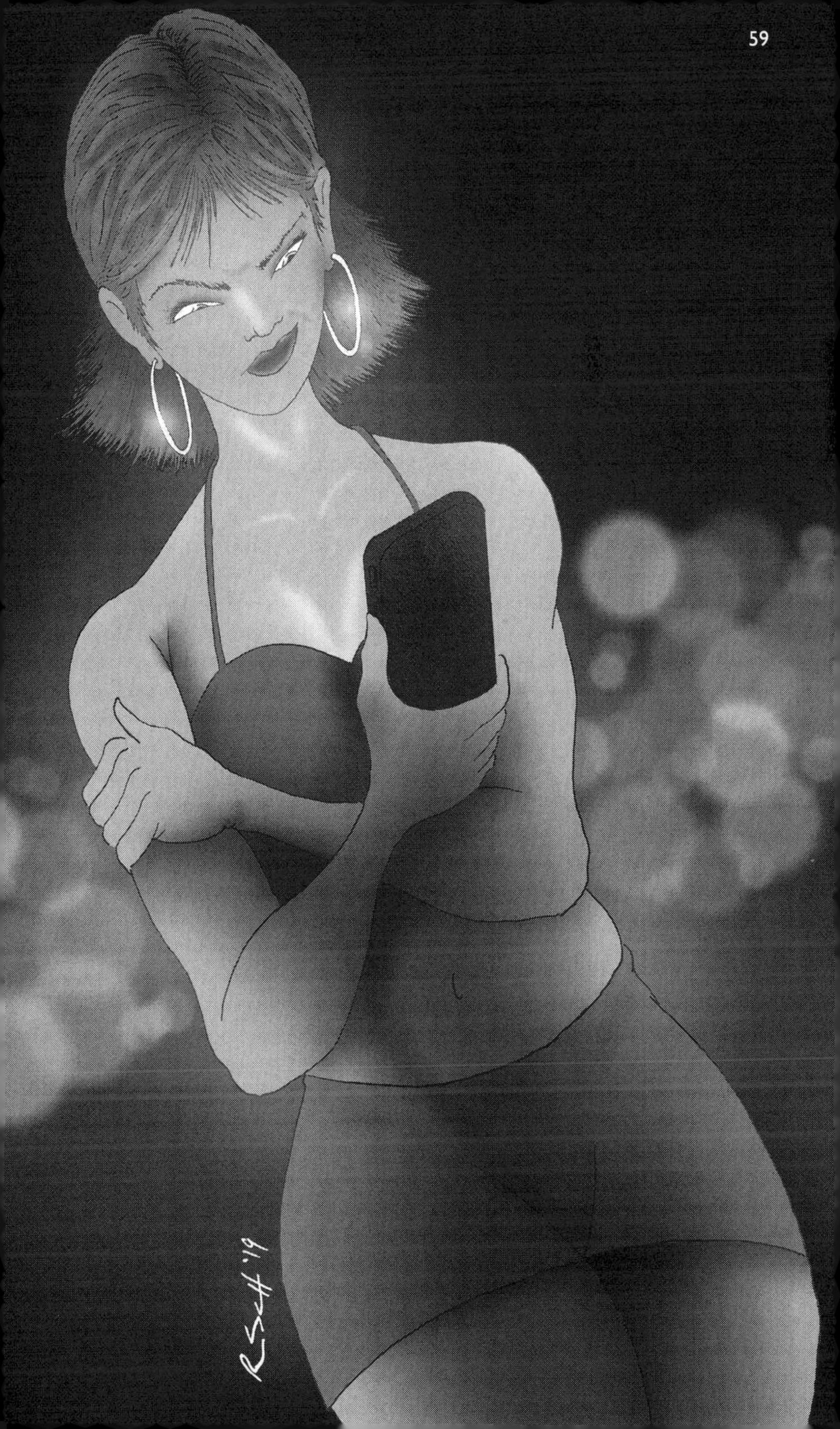

and its authoritarian methods mixed with socialism and a social credit system, many of the old problems were abolished or at least controlled. I used to be so proud of being the CFO of The Corp. How could I have been so stupid?

He had been researching tech history for a town hall company meeting when he found the top secret documents. They detailed buried research on cognitive issues being linked to mobile devices. He downloaded the files quickly onto a zip drive and mailed it to his niece before he could change his mind and rationalize the deceit. She was his only living relative and he wasn't close to her. In fact, he hadn't seen her since she was a little girl, even when she had reached out a couple years ago. He was incredibly busy and never got around to returning her texts or calls. He and his brother were estranged and hadn't talked in years. He hadn't even made it to the funeral when he and his wife were involved in that fatal hovercar crash. *That was an asshole move of me. Why hadn't I tried to meet her? Especially after her parents died? Too late now.* Taking another deep breath, he looked at the fairy dance floor, took a few steps back, and then launched himself off the roof.

Betty—The Lost Scientist

Betty woke up on the street lost and confused. It was cold, but she had a warm coat on. Pulling it close around herself, she shook her head trying to clear the fog from her brain. A large venting outtake blew warm air underneath her from the building she was leaning against.

She whispered to herself as she pulled herself up off the ground and looked around.

"My name is Betty and I know an important secret."

What was that thing she had to tell people about? Something about smart phones and radiation . . . Then the thought slipped out of her brain before she could finish it. She wasn't quite sure where she was, but she knew she was doing something crucial, something that might change lives. *She had been a lead researcher at The Corp but had been "offered" early retirement. She had started making noise about fears she had.* Running her hands down her body, she noticed this warm coat had pockets. Sticking her freezing fingers in them she pulled out a cell phone. On the screen there was a big notification:

LOST? CALL THIS NUMBER FIRST. 416-555-6781

Betty put the phone back in her pocket, she wasn't lost. She was on a mission. Brushing off the dirt on the seat of her flannel pajama bottoms, she took a look around at the deserted street and tall buildings. The sun was just rising up in the east over a big gorgeous lake. *Or was it the Ocean? No, she was pretty sure it was a lake, just what was it called?* She was going to be late for work. She was a scientific researcher . . . She wasn't sure where the office was, but a coffee would fix the fuzz in her brain. She started walking away from the water. *What was she looking for again? She was chilly and hungry.* What a beautiful old building up ahead! She stopped to gaze at the old stone and stained glass windows. Faded letters spelled out THE CATHEDRAL CHURCH OF ST. JAMES. Pushing on the old wooden doors, they opened and she walked into the enormous building. The light trickling through the coloured glass took her breath away. She couldn't see anybody around so she went to one of the long wooden benches and laid down for a nap.

Honour—The Legal Prostitute

Honour looked up at the ceiling muttering, "Oh ya' baby that's great."

She was counting the thrusts of her early morning client, hoping he would hurry up so she wouldn't be late for class. Working as a legal prostitute wasn't a great choice for a part-time job, but she could make the most amount of money in the least amount of time. Plus, the hours were flexible enough for school. Her parents died in a car crash a year ago, just as she was finishing high school.

Unfortunately, her dad had been more concerned with creating art pieces than saving money. He dreamed of becoming a renowned and rich creator of selfie environments. This art phase started about twenty years ago and had become a mainstay for museums in every metropolitan city. But sadly, he remained a starving artist. They subsisted off of her mother's construction worker paychecks. Enough for the basics, but her mom had two dependants. They lived hand to mouth.

Honour tried to get in touch with her rich Uncle Frank, the CFO of The Corp. She hoped he could help her cover university tuition, but he never returned her texts or calls. A package arrived that morning with a little zip drive in it from him, but she hadn't had a chance to look at it yet. She didn't need data files, she needed Corpcoin.

When Dave was done, he hopped off her and threw his jeans and t-shirt on. Honour knew he was married and loved to complain that his wife "didn't get him."

She didn't like Dave's uber-male persona and felt sorry for his wife, but his digital currency was as good as any and he passed all the state-mandated health standards. When he left her apartment, she went to the window and looked down at the early morning view. She saw a lady wandering down the street looking like a toddler; not sure which direction her feet were going to take her, pausing to catch her balance. From her fifth-floor apartment she couldn't make out her age, or if she was in trouble. She thought about running down to see if she could do anything, but by the time she got dressed and hit the streets, the woman would probably be out of sight. Anyways, this new and modern city had cameras everywhere. A patrol would pick her up.

Betty sighed. The momentary distraction of the confused walker left her to confront how she always felt after a session with a client. Self-revulsion choked her. She needed money, but didn't she also need her soul? Every time she let some stranger climb into bed with her, she felt as though a piece of her died.

Isla—The Rescue Worker

Isla started her shift at 7.00am and was scanning through the security cam notifications when she saw one marked urgent. She opened the webcam and saw the older woman walking on the sidewalk in the business district in a jacket, pajamas and slippers. Every few minutes she would stop and look around. Finally, she walked into the historical building that used to be an old church before the majority of the population abandoned organized religion. Probably a dementia case who wandered away from home. Isla opened a dialogue box and sent out a request to have her picked up. At least she would be safe and warm in the old Cathedral until a patrol could reach her.

Homelessness used to be a rampant social problem, but real progress had been made in the last twenty years. Isla worked in the social services division of The Corp and kept an eye on the city. Sort of a preventative 9-1-1 service.

Isla logged onto her social media site on HomePage and posted, "another woman will sleep in a warm bed tonight because of The Corp's vigilance!" She posted almost every work accomplishment and personal activity on her feeds. HomePage was her personal bible, journal, and most important communication tool. Though she had several thousand on-line friends, a breeze of loneliness was always drafting over her.

Isla didn't see any new alerts on her cameras, so she opened her Corp Love Connections App to re-read her messages from Samar. She had a real-world date tonight with him. Actual live human interaction could be the cure to her blues. They both swiped right a couple weeks ago. They texted and chatted like they'd known each other forever. Samar regaled her with intense tales of his homeland, India. She especially loved the stories he told of spirituality and how they practiced the Hindu religion. He defected here on a business trip a year ago and would have loved to find a girlfriend and settle down. His own Goddess Parvati.

Angus—The Alcoholic Paramedic

Angus was startled awake by his automatic blinds at 7.30am. They flapped up at the same time every day, he should have been used to it. He had not slept well, dreaming about the confused lady he had picked up yesterday from downtown core. She was suffering from delusions and may have been schizophrenic.

"Don't abduct me! I don't want to be prodded by aliens again!"

The memory of her voice still careened around his head, and he wanted to bury into his covers, not get up. The in-house

Artificial Intelligence, ARISA winked its red camera eye from
the ceiling above his studio's front door.

"You have slept for five hours and had three REM disruptions.
Your blood pressure and pulse are elevated, Angus. Plus, it
seems you drank enough alcohol to breach the maximum
allowable amount last night when you had me off-line."

Angus took a deep breath. "Morning ARISA."

"You should not be drinking quite so much, you are in
Hypertension Stage One. You have a 3.54% greater chance of
having a heart attack. Based on you being informed, your health
insurance will be void if you have a cardiac episode today."

Angus rolled out of bed, trying not to grab his head and give
away the fact he had a pounding headache.

"Thanks ARISA, I'll be skipping my CrossFit workout this
morning. Nothing to worry about. Glorious day!"

"Angus don't try and distract me with the weather. I am
concerned. If you continue to drink more than the maximum
allowed amount of alcohol, you will be remanded to a treatment
center. You are also losing a social credit for every poor
beverage choice."

Angus pulled on his standard white uniform and got ready
to go pick up his first "client." He tried not to be too irritated
by the loss of social credits. This was a system originally used
in communist China in the early 2000's. High social credit
ratings helped you get upgrades in your vehicles, housing, and
entertainment vouchers.

"Got it ARISA, no drinking tonight, put yourself on privacy
setting please."

"As you wish."

He hoped he hadn't triggered any warning signals in the
system. He'd had a couple of stints in the treatment centers, and
he didn't need more group therapy and nutritional advice. He
divorced one nagging wife and then The Corp started putting
AI's into all new condo building units. Maybe it was time to
move. If only he could divorce ARISA.

Nothing ever really went the way he wanted it to. Angus had
gone to school to be a content creator, but as soon as he was in
his thirties, he noticed a change in the attitude to him at work.

The Corp's business model called for young, cheap workers. Luckily, they funded many retraining programs and had been sending new career ideas to him on his feed. He saw there was a need for paramedics in the Community Aid division and it paid the bills while distracting him from liquor and beer. At least it was better than sitting in an office all day.

Of course, he didn't own a vehicle himself. You have to earn a shit-ton of carbon credits and social credits before being eligible to own a personal hovercraft. Angus had to use a push-pedal hover bike to get to work. He stumbled down the stairs to the basement to get his cycle off of the automated storage carousel. It took most of his concentration to keep his bike upright and moving in an almost straight line, when a pretty woman ran across the path. Angus swore and almost toppled when he swerved to avoid her.

"Hey Chubb! Get out of the way, you Pastry Puff!" Angus shouted.

Ouch, he must be crankier than he thought—way too much whiskey last night and shouting made his head pound even harder.

Emily—The Cheating Wife

The minutes couldn't tick by fast enough. Emily was meeting her lover. Just because her lover happened to be a woman made everything a bit more exciting. Her husband Dave was so crass, so rough, and Darlene was the opposite. Soft hands, soft voice. She loved being with her.

She rushed out of the office as soon as it was quitting time. She worked the night shift at The Corp creating clickbait lists. Without looking she charged across the exercise path, her sights set on the coffee shop across the road where they always started their rendezvous. Just a couple of ladies having Cappuccinos.

"Hey Chubb! Get out of the way, you Pastry Puff!"

The cyclist was powering down the path using rage to fuel his locomotion. Emily jumped out of his way, shocked at his insult. *Chubb? Pastry Puff?*

She was a perfectly normal looking 40-year-old woman. A few extra pounds maybe, but really not fat. God, she hated men. At least, some men.

Pushing through the doors of the coffee shop, she saw Darlene at their usual table and was so happy to see her she couldn't resist leaning in for a quick kiss. Those lips and blonde hair. She was so beautiful.

Too bad she didn't notice the nosy fellow at the next table surreptitiously take a photo and post it on his public feed. When she got home, her husband was waiting, and he was not happy.

Dave—The John and Abusive Husband

"Do not leave your unit Dave Trumbull. The Corp Patrol have been notified and will be around to pick you up for questioning. Domestic violence is strictly forbidden." The ARISA in his apartment winked its red eye and informed him in her melodious voice.

Dave picked himself up from the couch he collapsed on after giving his wife a quick crack across the face. He couldn't believe he did it. His insides were so full of burning rage, his skin was cooking on his hot bones. Emily cheated on him. Some distant cyber friend of his snapped a photo of "two hot lesbians" at a cafe and he recognized his wife.

He and his buds back in college used to joke about how great it would be if their girlfriends wanted to get it on with another girl. Now that he was living it, it wasn't great at all. Maybe if he hadn't found out along with the rest of the world on social media, he would have reacted differently. Even worse, the condo AI caught his little slap to her face and now there was clear evidence he had hit his wife.

He activated his iWrist and called his lawyer.

"Chuck, hello. Ya'. I saw the post on Homepage. Ya', that's what I'm calling about. I may have given her a little love tap when she showed up at the apartment this morning."

Dave listened for a bit. His lawyer explained to him that he wouldn't be going to jail. First time offenders get rehabilitation services, counselling and a fee punishment. The anger management classes are held at old churches. Since the historical buildings are no longer used for weekly worship sessions, they have been retrofitted as community classrooms.

This system lessened repeat behaviour and actually helped people get better rather than locking them up with criminals who either abused them or taught them how to be better criminals.

"Thanks Chuck. Can you meet me at Corp Patrol processing? I'm pretty sure I am going to be picked up shortly and brought there. Okay. See you soon."

Samar—The Counsellor

Samar drove around with Angus in his hovercraft when they saw a new alert pop-up from headquarters. Victim of Domestic abuse needed help. Counsellors often rode with the paramedics and this was an incident that needed a sympathetic ear even more so than medical intervention. They drove to the reported area and saw a woman walking quickly down the sidewalk sobbing and holding her hand to her head. They pulled over and Samar got out with a blanket and started talking to her in a soothing voice.

"Ma'am we are here to help. Could you stop for a minute and let me render aid?" Samar gently laid the microfiber heating sheet on her and she turned and cried into his shoulder.

There was something about Samar's soft accent and kind demeanor that inspired trust.

Angus stood back and dropped his mouth in shock.

"It's you. The lady on the bike path. Are you okay?"

Samar gently removed Emily's hand from a very black and swollen eye. She shook her head and didn't seem to recognize Angus as the fellow bellowing names at her earlier in the day.

Samar took her other hand and put a mug in it filled with hot chocolate and a mild sedative. He'd defected from India just a year ago. The streets were clean, and there was almost 100% employment in this new land, but it lacked the colour and passion of his home country. India was full of prayer, poverty, celebration, overpopulation, and lots and lots of life. Samar was willing to accept 24/7 monitoring and stop practicing his Indian religion for the chance to send desperately needed money back to his family.

"What's your name love?" Samar asked the woman as he helped her get into the van.

She stopped crying and looked over at Angus.

"Pastry Puff apparently. But when I'm not being screamed at by mad cyclists, I go by Emily."

"I'm sorry that happened with my co-worker. Perhaps he needs sensitivity training. Where is your husband now?" Samar asked.

"He's in our apartment, and I don't really blame him. Who wants to see their wife making out with another woman over coffee on the internet? I hear my post is viral."

Samar sat down beside her in the hovervan.

"Yes, your information file included that. We will take you for processing and then get that eye looked at by a doctor. Do you have any family you can stay with?"

"Only my grandparents, Betty and Darryl Bowmeister. But my grandmother is in the early stages of Alzheimer's. I'm not sure if my grandfather can handle another body in the house."

Samar consulted his chart and saw Betty Bowmeister's name on his patient pick-up list from this morning.

"Emily. You won't believe this, but we just picked up your grandmother earlier today at the St. James Cathedral. We will see her at central processing."

Betty—The Lost Scientist

Betty sat on a couch in central processing with a nice warm drink in her hand. The taste was so familiar. She remembered it from childhood. What was it called? She usually liked it with marshmallows. Oh yes. Hot Choco. She loved Hot Choco. Why was she here?

"Grandma! How are you! Oh my goodness, are you okay?"

A lovely lady with red hair and a swollen black eye hugged her. What a wonderful smelling lady, and the warm arms around her neck felt comforting.

"I'm fine. Just remembering what it was like worshiping at a church. I have very clear childhood memories. But what happened to you dear? Who are you and why is your eye all puffed up like that?" Betty asked the lovely lady.

"Grandma, it is me Emily. Dave and I had a fight. I heard they found you on the street, apparently you were going to work in your pajamas?" Emily said, trying to smooth Betty's rumpled hair.

"I have some very important information dear. It's about people's safety. I just need to remember . . . I must get there now. If you will excuse me, I have to find headquarters." A frown creased Betty's face as she got up and headed for the door.

"Sit back down for a minute Grandma. Do you recognize me? Emily. Your granddaughter," Emily gently took her elbow.

"I'm not old enough to have grandkids dear! And I do have to be getting to work."

Emily looked at her grandmother in frustration as she guided her back down onto the seat. She reminded herself it's not Betty's fault she can't remember things.

"Oh, yes, this is a really nice drink." Betty took a sip of the hot chocolate she'd rediscovered in her hand. "It was my favorite as a child. With marshmallows."

Samar came over and joined Emily and Betty with a warm smile. He asked Emily to walk into a little room with him and invited her to sit in an armchair.

"Betty won't be going home Mrs.Trumbull. We found her lost on the streets three times. Three is the magic number. Now she is going to one of our special facilities for society members with dementia. Corpcare Town is really amazing."

Samar popped open a laptop and showed her a digital pamphlet. "It is set up as an old-fashioned town and patients live in a non-confrontational safe environment. We don't force them to confront reality, instead, we let them enjoy their delusions and beliefs. Can you help gather memorabilia, photos and some of her favorite stories for us? We will decorate her 'house' with them to help as memory triggers."

A look of relief crossed Emily's face. "Of course I can. There have been reports about how highly successful your treatment towns are. I'm looking for a new job and would not mind working where my grandmother is going. Working with people who can't remember the latest Homepage feed update may be a refreshing change."

"There is a retraining program available and elder care is a growing segment of the economy. Let me see if I can get you hooked up. Part of the reason I left India for the Connected Colonies is the 100% employment stats of those that can work," Samar said.

"You came from India? Wow. I have seen crazy footage online and on the news stations. So polluted, so many sick and unemployed. But the culture seems vibrant and gorgeous," Emily said, happy to focus on someone else's story.

"Yes, my people are fascinating, amazing, and free. But here in the Connected Colonies, there is next to no pollution, very little crime, and everyone has a job and is taken care of. The lack of privacy takes getting used to, but I think personal privacy is a price we are willing pay for safety and opportunity. At least that is a price I was willing to pay," Samar said.

Honour—The Legal Prostitute

Computer Coding and Technological Sciences was a great choice for future employment prospects but could be mind-numbingly boring to learn. Honour staggered back into her apartment and collapsed on her couch. What she really wanted was a glass of wine, but the in-house ARISA monitored everything consumed and she didn't want her social credits or health statistics to be affected. Instead, she brewed some mint tea and finally slipped the zip drive from her Uncle Frank into her home computer. *Oh my god, what was this?*

It looked like a report on how the radiation from the new super powerful smart phones was causing cognitive failure. Dementia numbers were rising in the population. Honour loved reading all the latest scientific articles that popped up on her feeds, and she had never heard a peep about this. *How many hours a day did she have her phone glued to her head?* It even stayed tethered to its charger on her bedside table. She was moving that to another room post-haste. Could this be true? She had seen all the ads for Corpcare Towns. The date on this research was a couple of years old, there must have been a cover up in action. The Corp made, sold, and created all content for smart phones. Someone at the Corp might have found the zip drive interesting. Somebody might have been willing to pay her a good amount of money to give it back and stay silent. A smile slowly spread across her face. She was going to call all her clients and tell them she was retiring. Then she was going to set up a meeting at The Corp. She was going to be rich, at least for as long as her memory lasted . . . .

Angelique Fawns is a speculative fiction writer with a day job producing promos for Global TV in Toronto. She lives on a farm north of the city with far too many animals including fainting goats, horses and a guard llama. You can find her work in the anthologies *Demonic Carnival*, *The Corona Book of Ghost Stories*, and *Ellery Queen Mystery Magazine*.

"I took a picture on my cell phone of the murderer."

We are all hustlers now. Expect the worst.

Three, Two, One Zebra-Stripe Shake-Off

J.D. Graves

WHEN THE OPAQUE panel slid back, the stink of a million nations perfumed the prison cell. Most of the twenty-three cell mates turned towards the opening as Assistant Warden Martha Black called out, "Inmate X975006, J. Rory Woodcock step forward."

For a moment, no one stirred. Then twenty-two inmates not
called looked away or returned to their card games, or brushed
their metallic teeth, one grunted and filled the slops tube, and
one fellated another while two others waited their turn, and
one removed dead scales from a blue/black Reptilian who
yawned a mouth full of razored teeth, and one tattooed strange
hieroglyphs on his arm, and others in this brood of horribles
busied themselves with limited physical exercise in the small
confines, and yet none stepped forward. Assistant Warden Black
commanded again. One wrapped on the bunk above him and a
blonde man rolled over.

This inmate groaned, "What song of six torments is this?"

A drotronic prison guard entered the hovel. Any inmates in its way cleared a wide path. Its treaded legs pushed its bulk towards the blonde man's bunk. A blue light radiated from the guard's facial scanner. It swiped sideways across the blonde's face gridding his features.

From the guard's speaker a feminine voice spoke, "Inmate X975006, Joseph Rory Woodcock. Terran National. Convicted 20.7.2319 by the supreme judges of Omnamb Corporation on Ossis Seven for the crimes of forgery and theft."

The drotronic guard's speaker crackled grimly, "Come with me now or suffer force."

Rory Woodcock showed his palms, "I'm coming you gear bucket—don't zap me. I ain't spending another week in the infirmary."

Outside the cell the opaque panel closed behind them.

Assistant Warden Black smiled, "You have a visitor."

"I already told you hacks, I don't wanna' see no one."

"Trust me Inmate X975006," said the Assistant Warden, "you'll want to meet with this one."

The middle-aged woman proceeded down the endless corridor. The drotronic guard gave Rory no choice but to follow. They passed countless rounded cell windows. Rory thought, *Why won't these credit-hunters leave me be. Don't they know I'm locked up and can't pay back what I owe?*

Rory glanced and saw raucous activity thud against the glass window, faintly making out arms and legs in struggle. The drotronic guard's speaker crackled, "Hold please."

"If you must—be quick about it." She folded her arms, annoyed.

The guard crackled mechanically, "Stand back inmate."

Rory pressed against the far wall. Anytime the guards used electro-magnetic pulse it stirred bad memories. The cell panel opened. Shouts and two swinging inmates spilled into the corridor.

The guard gave no warning as an electrode touched the two scuffling men. Immediately, they released each other and convulsed on the floor. White foam leaked from their mouths. Inside the cell quieted. *Fresh meat,* Rory thought as the drotronic

guard reclosed the cell panel and left the inmates writhing on
the floor.

Rory lost count of how many more cell windows they passed.
Eventually they stopped and a window opened. A rather fey
man sat behind a chrome table. He wore an abundance of
jewelry and glamorous face paint. Rory at once took the man for
a fop.

"Go on," said his handler, "we'll wait outside."

Rory stepped through the orifice alone and it sealed behind
him. The fey man smiled warmly, "Rory Woodcock?"

Rory nodded at his new confines. One of the loaded rooms the
prison used to correct poor behavior. No guards needed—any
activity and the eye in the sky tripped the sensors. The fey man
stood and held out a hand, "Octavius Brown, Recruiting Officer
Guck Dynamics Corporation."

Rory eyed the extravagant hand suspiciously. He'd heard
of rich travelling faggots who toured intergalactic prisons
shopping for rough trade. They'd bribe wardens with pos-creds
then slip prisoners a mind-altering mickey before sodomizing
them. *This guy*, Rory thought, *looks just like that kind of faggot.*
Rory refused to shake hands and said, "If you're looking for
a quality cheap thrill I ain't worth it . . . I got anal chlamydia
or some shit, the medic don't know what—but I gotta' apply
a pungent cream morning and night to stop the blisters from
burning my brown eye."

The fey man paused before honking with laughter. "I can
assure you, neither I nor my employer . . . let's just say I've seen
plenty of zebras on this safari and you're not even worth
a picture."

"Yeah," Rory grated, "betcha' say that to all the boys."

"Does that bluff work on your cell mates? I have read your
medical file and you possess no such symptoms or diseases."

"Just got diagnosed," Rory said, unable to help himself.

The fey man frowned. "Years in the punitive system taught
you to be cautious and I respect that. I bare you no ill will or
harm. So, please have a seat so we can get down to the real
business of this visit."

"Can ya' hurry this along? I need back in my cell."

The fey man wrinkled his nose, "I've never met a prisoner so determined to stay imprisoned."

"I'm trying to put in my minutes. Only three days away from having enough for an hour of fresh air outside. I want my hour—I earned it."

The fey man grinned wolfishly and leaned forward, "What if I told you that you could breathe fresh air today?"

Rory looked him over queer. A multitude of outrages ran the gauntlet of his imagination. Whatever this fag wanted, he knew it wouldn't hurt to hear him out. Rory slowly sat.

The fey man asked, "Tell me everything you know about colonization."

Rory grimaced. "Hell . . . I'd rather take a Quintzel's meat hammer up the rump than join the colonies. I ain't no Chrixlam freak looking to convert savages."

The fey man beamed, "Yes, that is a common reaction. There's quite a bit of misinformation and rumor surrounding the practice. Ones my employer and I hope to remove as we go forth with our newest project."

"Project? Is that what ya' call stranding humans off world?"

"My employer and I have no intentions of stranding anyone anywhere. Plans are in action. We shall join the colony with our corporate headquarters just as soon as it is feasible."

"Why ain't it feasible now?"

"We need bodies, Mr. Woodcock," He licked his lips. "We are prepared to offer you a generous package of benefits including a full pardon for all transgressions."

Rory squinted at the man, "How did I get so lucky?"

"My employer believes in the goodness of humanity. Despite eons of technological achievements, human beings remain the same emotional creatures whose frailties and ambitions drive their advancement. There's nothing more extraordinary than a man facing adversity. Now, our company does not condone the stealing of corporate secrets for sale on the black market of which you were found guilty. And you may not believe in the principles of Chrixlam, but my company does. We're offering you forgiveness."

Rory shifted in his seat. "I've heard of things like this. Lemme' guess, you're using the Chrixlam as some cover . . . your company owns the mineral rights to some planet, but the locals ain't interested in assimilating . . . And since the Association banned the use of drotronic soldiers, ya'll need an army to clear the competition for resources . . . that about right?"

The fey man sniffed. "Our project already has a heavy military installation . . . what we lack are families."

Rory laughed, "Ain't gonna' find 'em in places like this."

"No," Mr. Brown nodded. "But we will find half of the essential ingredients."

Rory's smile faded. "Where ya' finding the other half?"

"Places where forgotten ladies can earn a living . . ." He clucked his tongue. "The old-fashioned way."

"You're filling your colonies with whores and prisoners?"

"We are offering a marginalized population a fresh start and unburdening the Association with undesirables."

The fey man swiped across a tablet in front of him. A hologram of a blue sphere materialized. "This is Jubilation, a class two planet similar to your native Terra. There are over four thousand discovered species of unique fauna and flora, all cohabitating on three sizeable continents."

"What about the natives . . . the one's at the top of the food chain?"

"The Chiznaks? A backwards cave dwelling folk who worship water . . . but not really a problem . . . there's plenty of room for everyone on Jubilation."

Rory sat back in his chair. He'd learned long ago, opportunity only knocked once. Sixteen years of a twenty-year grind still lay ahead of him. He detested sharing a cell with those goombas, brutes, and pederasts. But at least he knew he'd stay alive. Colonists' life expectancies couldn't be determined — too many variables. But even then, there was nothing saying he couldn't escape once his transport touched down.

Rory smiled. "Sure, I'll join up on one condition."

Octavius brightened. "And that is?"

"Does my file say anything about my debts?"

The fey man nodded slowly and said, "I suppose you want us to write a guaranty for the balance?"

"It's only fair, don't you agree?" Rory smiled.

"Getting your freedom back isn't good enough?"

Rory shook his head, "How free can someone be if he's lugging a millstone of debt around his new homeland?"

Octavius rubbed his chin, "It's highly unorthodox. It would take approval from the board of directors, but just between me and you . . . they're desperate for bodies. They'll probably agree."

Rory's heart soared like a rocket. He couldn't believe it. All he'd needed to do now was plan his escape. His excitement dipped slightly as Octavius swiped across the tablet. A woman's face replaced the hologrammed planet.

"I'm so glad we can agree to terms Mr. Woodcock," Octavius's bared his teeth. "I'd like to introduce you to your new wife."

"My new what?"

"I guess the correct term is fiancé." Octavius laughed. "Her name is Autumn Line."

All the air rushed from Rory's lungs. He sat there like a lump staring at the hologram flickering in and out of focus. Chumps are content with being fooled as long as they don't realize it. He'd been lied to plenty of times before now, but none stung quite like this.

"She's twenty-three." Octavious smiled. "Which is a bonus."

"Yeah . . ." Rory muttered. He wanted to rage.

"Is something the matter?" Octavious leered at him.

What was Rory supposed to say? This ponce had him dead to rights. Bait the hook with freedom and pull. Rory wondered how many others this sales pitch had snagged. *Keep your mind on your business and first chance we get we take care of it.*

He smiled. "She's a fine girl . . . I'm sure she'll make me very happy."

Rory signed a few forms. And the next thing he knew, he stood in a long line of around twenty other volunteers. No need for manacles—not for newly freed men on the edge of the desert. They loaded onto a low gravity shuttle and sped across the wasteland. Inside the cabin, rumors swirled in whispers. Already talk turned to escape amongst the freed men.

"When opportunity knocks," said a dark man, "I'm opening the door."

Another answered, "Yeah, I hear Chrixlam makes you wear

magic underwear—cuts off all desire to frag."

"Some kind of mind control."

"Why would they give us a wife if that were true?"

"They ain't given us nothing," cried a thief. "They're selling us into the institutional slavery of marriage."

"Who knows how old those holograms are? Those bitches could weigh twenty-two stone—fat from eating whore's rations."

"Ain't so bad," drawled a con man. "Big girls can give as much pleasure as one of them three-credit-skinners with the vibrating holes . . . if you know what I mean."

Another laughed, "You know why fat women eat a good wonk? Because they have too!"

More laughter erupted in the shuttle's cabin.

A larger man said, "Those skinners can be quite realistic. I had one attach her ass to me for an entire week before I got wise. Afterwards, that cybortic bitch tried to cut my throat. Those machines are tough to kill, but not impossible."

"You must be dumber than a clock's hand." The con man laughed. "Her silicone ports didn't give her away?"

"It was her eyes. They got them mismatched colors with tiny Q codes woven into the web of the corona. When I stomped her in, I felt no remorse."

Octavious Brown shook his jewelry at the men knowingly and smiled. "Those pleasure machines are an abomination. The faith and the company frowns on all uses of them. I advised you all to remember that once we arrive."

"Chrixlam City got a cybortic whore problem?"

Octavious Brown smiled. "By heavens no. Prostitution is punishable in all Chrixlam districts. I'm afraid our faith's openness has caused a refugee situation. Just not enough room for everyone and so some must be released."

"Refugee? Released?" Rory asked. "You mean . . . ?"

"I'm afraid the Architect doesn't allow humanoids created outside his blueprints."

"Hey Autonomous Brown," the dark man said, "will we get to meet our wives before we're married off?"

"Everything in due time," the fey man said. "To make suitable wives they attend a separate female only orientation. One last rigorous test of their new dedication to the faith."

The last words rung hollow in Rory's ears.

The shuttle landed. The freed men stepped out. A man in purple robes welcomed them heartily. "May the Architect bless each and every soul today. I am Cornell and I welcome you to the Institution of Brotherhood. Here you shall learn of the Architect's plan and your own place amongst the infinite."

One by one, the freed men entered a room lined with desks and purple robed receptionists. Here, these workers scanned the former prison inmate's vitality microchips. Then they moved on. In an even larger hall, Rory and the others gathered themselves in rows. Already, you could smell the stink of a thousand jails. Gentle yet sparse music filled the space as hundreds upon hundreds of men seated themselves before a variegated wall.

The doors closed. The lights dimmed. The show began.

A cavalcade of oaths strobed across the walls and echoed through the sound system. The Three Foundations of Chrixlam:

"I believe in free will and the eternal soul. I believe in the exceptionalism of man. I believe in the Architect of the universe. I believe in free will and the eternal . . ."

On and on it went for what seemed like hours. A volunteer from another jail tired of the cult's show and started to leave. He made it as far as the door before a member of the Brotherhood caught him. A negotiation ensued. Screams barely registered above the droning mantras. Rory and the others bleated along with the other sheep, the Twenty-Seven Temptations and How to Thwart Them. The Ten Chrixlam Psalms of Intergalactic Travel and Inner Peace. No one else dared to flee.

One man, twenty rows in front, ecstatically screamed and stood — arms and legs shivered in wild gyrations. Rory's neck hair prickled as the strange arrhythmic dance spread to one, and then another, and another. Rory feared if he didn't play along he'd be singled out. *Was this the rigorous tests the fag had promised? Would the Brotherhood notice him faking it?*

It continued on and on. No way to track time. Rory's legs ached and his head filled with enough air to lift off his body. They weren't allowed to sleep. This pattern repeated itself for three more days. No food. No water. Just three exhausting

mind-numbing slogs of singing and kneeling and praying.
Thoughts of escape too, began to disappear. He felt like a boat
adrift at sea. Unable to impose his will against the waves.
On the fourth day or maybe not, a woman took the podium.
Her face projected in every direction on every surface of every
wall. She wore a white veil and purple jump suit. Even through
the stink of a thousand men, her soft flowery scent wafted
through the air. Her sweet voice echoed in the hall.

"Good morning brothers, I am Sister Agatha. I know you
are ready to meet your future forever companion. But before
we complete the Architect's design—gentlemen you must
understand the Five Demands of a Chrixlam husband."

More inane repetitions. *Husbands must love and be faithful
to their wives.* The smell of flowers brought Rory back to his
childhood. *Husbands must provide the family with social, body,
and financial security.* He could see fields of yellow daffodils.
Husbands must establish a joint fund of property to benefit children.
He felt the sensation of running barefoot. *Husbands must lead the
family in the ways of Chrixlam and be just in resolving conflict.* Rory
could almost see his former identity vanishing into a past that
never existed. *Husbands must be paragons of Chrixlam virtue. Be
kind. Be firm. Be infinite.*

Rory yammered along, unsure if there'd ever been anything
before Chrixlam City. It seemed to Rory he'd always been at the
Institution of Brotherhood. Everything before seemed like a
false memory or a dream. Decades flew by in an instant. He'd
always been here, sure. He believed in free will and the eternal
soul. He believed in the exceptionalism of man. He believed in
the Arch—

A voice boomed, "When we call your name, come down the
aisle and join your bride in honored matrimony."

Rory looked around and didn't recognize the place. Large
floor to ceiling stained glass windows glowed and refracted
the light. He didn't recognize the clothes on his body. A purple
jump suit with his name above the Chrixlam circle and ex logo.
Across the aisle sat row after row of white veiled women. Their
heads bowed dutifully. Rory started to stand. A hand reached
out and grabbed his wrist, "What do you think you're doing?"

"I dunno'," Rory said and meant it.

The voice leaned closer. "Sit back down you fool, or they'll ship you back to the prison in an incineration bag. You've already tried this once and failed."

"Failed?" Quickly Rory glanced around. A black clad brother with a visor looked his way. Rory convulsed with faux ecstasy and sat back down. "Whaddaya' mean I already tried once?"

"Four nights ago, you made a break for the door . . . you didn't get far."

"Four nights? That would be the first night wouldn't it?"

"We've been here two weeks now." The voice shook his head. "The key is to not draw attention to yourself. Not until you're through the transportal and on planet Jubilation."

Rory couldn't place the man. It seemed he'd known him from somewhere. "Transportal?"

"You really don't know what's going on? They're gonna' marry us off. Tie us to the whore with some kind of magic shackle . . . then push us through time and space to another planet. Whatever they did to you during their negotiations really messed you up, huh?"

"I . . . I . . ." Rory stumbled for words.

"Don't sweat it kid. This place had me going for a couple of days too. Lost all sense of everything. But I'm back now . . . just in time it seems. First chance I get . . . I'm peeling off."

Rory still couldn't place the man, but he seemed friendly enough. A name was called out, but Rory didn't catch it. The friendly man stood and walked down the aisle towards burning incense and a white veiled woman and a cone hatted brother. Some words were spoken and then . . .

"Joseph Rory Woodcock . . . Autumn Line, please come forward."

Rory stepped into the aisle and was met by his future bride. She didn't look up, keeping her head bowed to the floor. Her hands hidden, clasped together beneath her clothes. They marched side by side to the front where the cone hatted brother smiled. "Brother and sister. Do you Rory vow to uphold your wedding oaths and the Five Demands of a Chrixlam husband?"

Rory nodded.

"Do you, Autumn, vow to uphold your wedding oaths and the

Thirteen Sacrifices of a Chrixlam wife?"

Autumn nodded silently.

The cone hatted brother poured grey liquid into a gold cup of which he sipped and handed to Rory. Rory looked at his reflection in the grey liquid and didn't recognize it. The cone hatted brother cleared his throat. "Is there something wrong Brother Rory?"

Rory shook his head and sipped and held it out for his bride to drink. She finally looked at him, with terrified eyes. The cone hatted brother scowled. "Are you sure there's nothing the matter Brother Rory? Don't you remember Accelerated Wine is forbidden for women to drink?"

Confusion wrinkled Rory's face. In the periphery, he saw two black clad brothers stirring with long batons at the ready. Panic crept up Rory's spine. He started to speak, and mercifully his bride spoke first, "Forgive me Father Carlyle for speaking out of turn, but I think my new husband is just nervous. He meant no offense with his offer of a drink."

"Nervous?" Father Carlyle spat out the words. Then a wide grin wizened his face and a hearty laugh erupted. "Nervous! The boy's nervous!"

The laughter spread to those in close proximity.

"I'm certain your new bride will be most helpful in relieving any nerves you may have. I now pronounce you Husband and wife. Wear your newlywed bracelets with pride and good luck. Next couple!"

Rory's bride took his hand and a black clad brother clapped golden manacles on them both, one to the other. Rory walked out of the side door chained to this strange woman, unaware of what to do next.

Outside the cathedral the closest star set in the distance. The woman took his other hand. She pulled him close, "I need you to kiss me . . . now."

Rory paused.

She pleaded, "They are watching us. Kiss me or we'll both be in trouble."

Again, Rory paused. His bride lifted her veil and for the first time he got to see her. It felt like the first day of his life. She had two almond eyes, pink pouts for lips. Cheek bones that could launch a thousand ships and give every sailor a reason to reach dry land. She leaned forward and found his mouth with hers. Everything came rushing back to Rory. His new bride smelled clean, almost antiseptic. She pulled away and Rory licked his lips.

She drawled, "I know this ain't the best situation for either of us. I think we should get more acquainted don't you?"

Rory looked at her and smiled. "Your hologram doesn't do you any justice. You're far prettier than I was led to believe."

His bride's lips arched into a frown, "Don't say things like that so loud." She glanced around quickly. She slid her hand into his and pulled him along the sidewalk into a courtyard. Several newlywed couples milled about getting to know each other mentally, spiritually, and biblically.

She pulled him to a stone bench and sat. Her hands ran across him. "I need you to pretend that you love me."

"I think there'll be a lot of that happening here in this courtyard today."

"You don't understand," she pleaded. "I've done a terrible thing."

"Don't be so down, beautiful." Rory smiled. "I'm certain I will have no trouble falling in love with–"

"Don't say that," she pleaded again. "I can't have you falling in love with me." She wrapped her arms around him and kissed him deeply. Rory's mind swam an ocean of confusion. Her tongue darted in and out of his mouth. It had been so long, Rory had forgotten what it was like to kiss a woman. The antiseptic smell intensified. And then he felt it. A short sharp vibrato pulsed through her teeth. He stiffened in her arms and pushed her away. Her face clouded over with shock and fear.

Rory couldn't believe it. "Y-y-you're not real."

She didn't look at him. "Please keep your voice down."

"What the hell?" Rory's rage built inside him.

"I am real . . . I'm sitting here with you now. Doesn't that make me real enough?"

Rory looked around the courtyard. A multitude of couples lay deep in each other's arms as the sunlight died. A cadre of black clad guards paced to and fro along the Cathedral's walls. The dark thought occurred to him, "You're not really Autumn Line are you?"

His bride looked at him with eyes the size of saucers and shook her head. "No."

Rory stood.

"Where are you going?"

"I have to tell one of the brothers."

Her silicone eyes welled with oily tears. "Please don't . . . that's a death sentence for both of us."

"Not for me," Rory said. "I'm innocent."

"And I'm not?" His bride cried. "You're right, I may not be Autumn Line . . . but I am innocent. I didn't mean to be born like this."

"You weren't born," Rory said quietly. "You were manufactured in a facility that also makes artificial limbs and other junk. You're a byproduct of some pervert's imagination. Some complex cure for loneliness. But you aren't real."

"You may be flesh and bone. And I may be synthetic on the outside, but . . ." She shook her head. "I believe in the soul."

"Skinner's can't have souls," Rory said. "It goes against your programming. From the looks of you, you're some pleasure model." Then he thought about it some more, "So, you stick your head in the lion's mouth hoping to hold on to one of its teeth unnoticed. You hear about the Guck Dynamics Colonization plans and Bingo-Bango-Bongo, here we are . . . chained together in some cult marriage."

"I still believe in the soul," She cried. "The exceptionalism of man. The Architect's–"

"You're a cold skinner," Rory said. "I knew something crazy was gonna' happen to me. It always does. Nothing's ever easy for old Rory J. Never has been, never will."

"Please sit down," His bride asked flat. "You're drawing attention . . ."

A black clad guard approached. "Is everything all right in the Architect's great plan for the end of this wonderful day?"

Rory clenched his teeth. He glanced at his bride and back at the guard. Then he smiled, "Just a swelling of my pride. My new wife was quite an expensive prostitute before she accepted the three tenants of foundation. She was just confessing her sins to me as she should and I guess . . . they got under my skin."

The guard smiled. "Forgiveness is the key to a happy marriage. Chrixlam states a man and woman should cling to one another. The two of you headed to Traxon Nine?"

Rory shook his head. "Jubilation."

The guard's face fell. "Then you should take care of one another. That place will test what you're made of, for sure." The guard bowed his head and said, "Please enjoy the rest of your happy day and good luck."

The guard moved on. As Rory watched him go, he connected the dots. He had indeed allowed his pride to get the better of him. *This was the best-case scenario.* A cybortic lifeform would be unable to form emotional attachments. There would be no real bonding between them. Which is just what Rory needed if he was going to successfully make a break for it.

His bride asked, "Why didn't you tell the guard about me?"

Rory smiled slyly. "What happened to the real Autumn Line?"

His bride winced. One eye was green, the other blue. Her lips moved. "I don't know. But I didn't do it."

"Sure you didn't."

"Found her lifeless body in an alley and swapped identification chips. If the Chrixlam Brotherhood found out about me they'd . . ."

"Release you?" Rory asked.

"Is that what they call an execution?"

"How would you go about killing something that isn't alive in the first place?"

"A number of ways . . . are you planning something?"

"Yeah," Rory said, "but not that . . . I have no intentions of telling anyone the truth about you. And you'll do the same for me."

She brightened. "Do you want to know my real name?"

"Keep your feels to yourself . . . no need for complications, if you can feel anything anyways. I don't plan on sticking around Jubilation long enough to plant roots, if you get what I'm saying."

His bride nodded slowly.

"Good. Now, it seems that we both want off this rock. This bracelet here says we're not going alone. So, to make the best of a bad situation, I say we keep each other's secrets, just like a real marriage. But do not doubt for one second my intentions. Everything about a skinner is fake, so I'm being as real as possible. You're programming is logical, so knock it off with that soul nonsense. I know that if threatened, you will do whatever it takes to ensure your own survival. In a way, that makes you as real as most women."

His bride leaned towards him. "You say such ugly things."

"I speak the truth. Now kiss me, the guards are watching."

CROSSING THE PORTAL reminded Rory of the orientation sessions. All bright lights and exhaustion. He didn't know what went through his bride's head, but he didn't care. Although at the apex of the transportal trip, she gripped his hand tight with anxiety. Instinctively, he squeezed back. The crossing lasted mere minutes and the pair emerged onto a dry plain without their shackles. Hundreds of other newlywed couples milled about in hungry confusion.

Rory had expected to see a town at least. Some kind of primitive structure. Instead, nothing but the elements. A few tried to escape back through the transportal, but the thing didn't respond and there were no control panels on this side. Rory suddenly knew the terrible truth about their newfound freedom.

Rory's bride heard the war whoops first. She pulled at Rory's arm desperate to flee. "We must go . . . now!"

Instinctively, Rory followed her away from the group. They neared a strand of half bent trees when Rory finally heard the hellish cries. He turned back to see the first rattle of spears pass through the crowd. Shrieks of women as the Chiznak savages rode them down atop their strange, galloping beasts. The fog of dust made the carnage almost impossible to watch.

She pulled again. "C'mon or they'll kill us too."

They abandoned the colonists to fend for themselves, heading for shelter in a distant forest. Rory didn't know how long they'd walked, but Jubilation's sun set above.

He leaned towards her. "I dunno' about you, but if I don't eat or drink something soon I will die."

"I don't need food or water to survive."

"Lucky girl," Rory said and saw a few mounds of scrub grass.

He dropped to his hands and knees and smelled it.

"What are you doing?" she asked.

"Do you know if these are poisonous?"

"Here," she said and squatted beside him. "I will test it."

Rory pinched off a handful and gave them to her. She munched on a few blades. She scowled and shook her head. Then she laughed, a terrible mechanical noise. It chilled Rory to the bone.

"What's so funny?"

"I was just thinking about how desperate I was to leave Chrixlam City because the danger was so great. And now . . ."

She didn't have to finish it. Rory understood completely. But just like a real woman, she went on anyway, ". . . it seems the tables have turned. You were going to leave me once we got here." Her head tilted slightly. "Do you still think that's a good idea?"

Rory swallowed the lump in his throat. "Don't you believe in the eternal soul and the architect's great design?"

She laughed again. "Of course. But you don't. I wonder how long you'll survive if I left you here?"

"You can't leave . . . We're married, remember?"

His bride's smile fell. "I suppose . . . even if no one's watching."

They wandered further into the bent-tree forest. Rory's mind raced with hunger and fear. He needed a new plan. He knew he needed her, more than she did him. *How could he convince her to stay?* At length, they came upon a field full on bulbous plants with black flowers, growing barely a foot off the ground.

"What do you make of these?" Rory asked.

His wife scanned the field and said, "These are some kind of poppy-like cactus."

"Are they edible?"

She smiled and nodded. "My files tell me their fruit is quite tasty."

"But what about the black flowers? Don't seem like no invitation."

"Merely a deterrent."

Rory bent over one of the round plants. They smelled all right. As soon as his fingers grazed the tough hide, a cloud of nettles erupted. Rory fell back coughing and rubbing his eyes. The pain unbearable. No matter how hard he rubbed, he could not clear them. The world went black. He felt warm blood leaking from his eyes.

He cried out, "Help!" There was silence. He cried again.

"I'll help you on one condition," said his wife softly.

He desperately cried, "Name it I'll do *anything!*"

She chuckled with menace. "Tell me my real name."

J.D. Graves is an author and playwright whose stage work has appeared at the New York International Fringe Festival and the FronteraFEST. His short fiction can be found in *Black Mask, Mystery Weekly, Switchblade, Broadswords & Blasters, Santa Cruz Weird, Breaking Bizarro, Tough Crime,* etc. He serves as the Editor in Chief of *Econoclash Review* and is currently writing a novel. J.D. lives in the woods with his wife and kids.

"I had to snuff him out, Boss.
He tried to shine a flashlight on me."

'Fame, what is it good for? Absolutely nothing ...'

15 Minutes
Don Stoll

NATALIA HAD LOOKED forward to her 15 minutes of fame on the assumption they would last 15 minutes. Yet, coming up on 15 days since those 15 minutes, she craved obscurity. Every day a stranger would call her name in the street or accost her as she shopped for arugula or jump off a bicycle at a red light to beg for a picture.

One morning she told her new boyfriend Wally that she wished the prophecy had correctly been of *only* 15 minutes of fame. He suggested pedantically that someone other than the great artist had uttered the celebrated words.

She studied the donuts behind the glass and tried to decide: glazed, chocolate, or maple? The boy waiting behind the counter for her and Wally to order blurted out "You're Natalia Chi . . . Chi–" and Wally, talking over her attempted denial, said "Chichova; Natalia Chicherova is someone else."

Hoping to distract the donut boy with a discussion of Natalia Chicherova, Natalia said, "What's her claim to fame?"

"Lots of cats," Wally said. "Names them after old movie stars: Matt Damon, Leonardo DiCaprio . . . And won't own females. Says they're all bitches."

"Is she the one who lives–"

"Foothills of the Sierra Nevadas with the ocean right below her house," Wally said.

Natalia forgave the interruption. Wally loved information so much that it had to spill out of him like he was a dam with cracks in it.

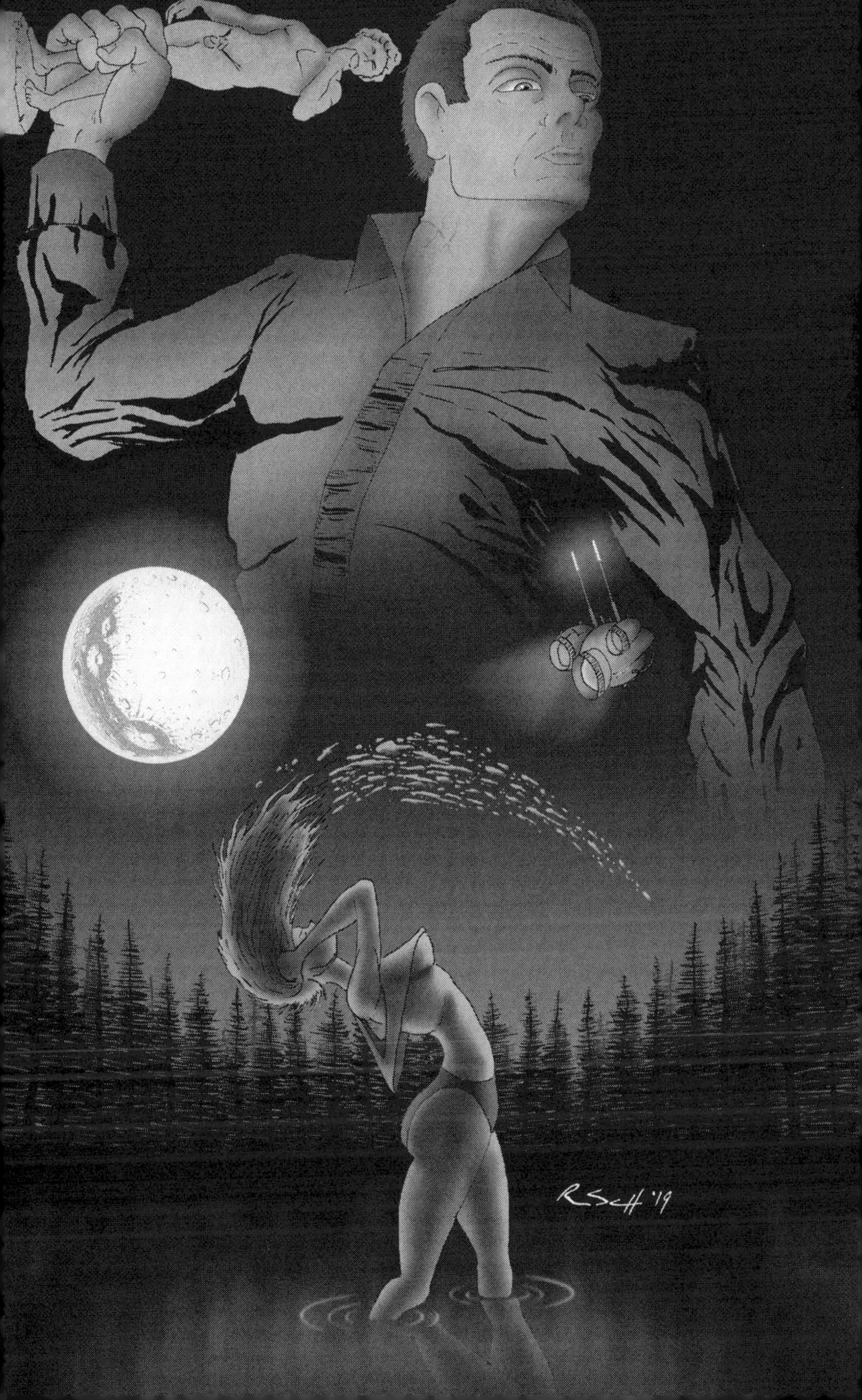
RSch '19

"Funny to think California used to have big cities," she said.

"Cool shoes," the donut boy said, nodding at the moccasins that Natalia considered too intricately beaded.

"Thanks," Wally beamed, oblivious to the mockery.

He had bought them off the feet of a homeless Anishinaabe man, begging on the streets of Minneapolis. Wally boasted of the "deal" he'd struck, but to Natalia the moccasins represented cultural appropriation and worse.

"Can I get a picture, Ms. Chi–"

"Chichova," Wally interrupted.

The boy insisted on selling the donuts at a discount.

"Nice kid, that Bobby," Wally said outside.

"Who?" Natalia said.

"The donut boy."

"How do you know his name?"

"I asked. You didn't hear him?"

She hadn't.

Wally rattled on about getting his breakfast for half-price. Natalia rolled her eyes, thinking *It's half-off four donuts and two lattes for God's sake.* She thought the donut boy's recognition of her and his demand for a picture had been a bad way to start the day. Though generally not inclined toward superstition, she also thought that it augured worse.

THE PEOPLE'S STATION (TPS) boasted that its 15-minute segments televised around the world had already made more than 50,000 people famous and that its ultimate goal was to give 15 minutes of fame to everyone on the planet. The least sophisticated critics of TPS pointed out that at the current pace bringing fame to everyone on the planet would take more than 200,000 years. More acute critics observed that this failed to take into account the billions of people who would die in obscurity before 200,000 years had elapsed. The founding CEO of TPS had refused to consider a reduction of the 15 minutes to 15 seconds despite the objections, reaching far back into history, which noted that Jack Ruby's live-TV killing of the killer of United States President John F. Kennedy had taken an instant. The CEO also insisted that true fame required exclusivity, hence she would never consider televising simultaneously on multiple channels. Critics argued that her vaunted exclusivity was a sham because viewers had countless other choices, anyway.

Changes were coming in the shape of well-funded competitors with TPS as well as, the rumors went, the CEO's ouster by her board.

But Natalia Chichova thought the numbers of people acquiring fame were already too large and as such had debased celebrity. If any randomly selected person could become famous, then the grounds of fame were likewise random. Reward for good was indistinguishable from punishment for evil and fame was indistinguishable from infamy.

The path to celebrity had opened up for Natalia less than a month before, right after she'd moved into her new apartment. In a bar on the next block she had met and begun an affair with the founder of one of the most successful bicycle sales-and-rentals companies in the Midwest. The delay by Minneapolis and St. Paul in outlawing cars had made banning them necessary, and her new man's response to the environmental crisis had won her heart. The research for her dissertation and all the research she'd done since suggested that environmental collapse was inevitable. But Natalia didn't believe in giving up.

As for her affair with a married man, that was morally indefensible. Yet, within the constraints of immorality, Natalia had comported herself with honor. She'd been unable to do otherwise because he had talked elaborately and endlessly about his wife and children. Despite having known Mark for barely a week, she felt like she'd known his wife, Edith, and their son and daughter her whole life. She had therefore worked scrupulously around Mark's commitment to attend Jimmy's soccer games and Shirley's ballet recitals. She'd worked around Edith's desire for a romantic weekend getaway to Banff to celebrate their twelfth wedding anniversary.

On the day Natalia would become famous, his wife and children were visiting her parents in Duluth. Natalia had no classes to teach and no papers to grade. She wouldn't demand his entire day—just a couple of hours. She would travel all the way across the city to his office. His job was demanding, but with his family away he could recoup the lost time by working late. After relaxing, he would work more effectively.

When she called, he put her on hold while he checked his day planner. He came back to give her two options: either 2:30 to 2:45, or 4:00 to 4:15. The sofa in his office meant they wouldn't have to leave. But she would need to show up primed for sex or their 15 minutes would be wasted. He hung up.

She called back and got his answering machine. At that moment the TPS HoverCam swooped into view and started televising her as she paced around Minnehaha Park. In her fury she talked throughout the 15 minutes of televising, long after Mark's machine had stopped recording. She stayed close to the spray of Minnehaha Falls. February in Minneapolis was mild. But she would get so worked up that after the HoverCam left she waded into a deserted part of the Creek in her underwear. Wally saw her emerging from the water and introduced himself.

"You looked like Botticelli's Venus," he would explain, "except you weren't naked."

Natalia tried to imagine the resemblance that Wally had seen between herself and Botticelli's Venus. Maybe he had a different painting in mind. His knowledge of art history was deficient and he wasn't rich, tall, powerfully built, and handsome like Mark. But he'd come along at the right moment.

Regarding her televised breakup with Mark, in retrospect Natalia would admit having played to the camera. The charm of celebrity wasn't lost on her even if it had become meaningless. Yet her anger was real. Perhaps she'd exaggerated the significance of the 15-minute thing. But was it mere coincidence that the 15 minutes of the TPS fame-making segments equaled the 15 minutes of the segments into which Mark had chosen to divide his life? Natalia didn't believe his job was so demanding that he could only tear himself away for 15 minutes. She thought Mark had simply become consumed by media—by other platforms in addition to TPS—and it was the media he couldn't bear separation from. She also thought that because TPS was the newest toy of media addicts, the idea of 15 minutes had taken on outsized importance.

So, there'd been her beef with the way the media had come

to occupy so much of our time with trivialities that we had
too little time left for important things like extramarital affairs.
And in her anger about being reduced to a sex object—You've
got 15 minutes, Mark had said, which will be all about sex—
Natalia had felt like a feminist hero, giving voice to the anger
of everyone belonging to her gender. Finally, she'd said
something to the machine about how the omnipresence of
media representations of the real world gave men one more
weapon with which to fight their tireless battle against intimate
engagement with other human beings.

"SPRING BREAK'S COMING," Wally said as Natalia tried
to ignore the way he was licking the maple frosting from his
second donut off his fingers. "How about if we both cancel class
that Friday and leave on Thursday afternoon for the Sierras?
We'll go way up north where they still get snow and rent a place
kind of midway up the slopes. That way I can go up to ski and
you can go down to the ocean."

"Want a napkin?" she said, unable to ignore the licking.

"Tongue works just as well," he laughed, wiggling his moist
fingers at her.

She didn't know about going to the Sierras with Wally. Unlike
Mark, he was willing to give her more than 15 minutes. But in
Minneapolis they had separate apartments. He had asked her
to move in with him—in her opinion going way too fast—and
she'd been grateful for the excuse that it would be a hassle to
move again after less than a month in her new apartment. What
if they went together and rented two different places? Why
suggest it, though, since he'd think it was weird?

"Sierras?" she said. "I'll think it over."

His face crumbled. Natalia wondered why he was so
insensitive to the historical predicament of Native Americans
and to her wish for basic courtesies, but so sensitive to any hint
that she wasn't passionate about him. She wondered how he
could teach psychology and yet have no insight into his own
psychology.

"Going back to my apartment to grade papers," she said.
"Have a good class. What are you talking about today?"

Outside her apartment a few minutes later she tried to remember his answer, but wasn't sure. Had he said he was going to lecture about sociopaths? She thought the Sierras might be a bad idea even if she could persuade him to rent two different places. Had she burned her bridges with Mark?

She headed for the bathroom to brush her teeth so that the acid produced by the sugar of the donuts wouldn't eat away at them. But she stopped halfway down the hall. Had she seen something out of the corner of her eye?

She went back to the front room. Mark was lying on the sofa.

"Wanted to surprise you," he said.

"How—"

"How'd I get in?" he said, but the gray shirt with his name stenciled on the pocket had already made her wonder why she'd never found it strange to have met him in a bar in a part of the city far from where he worked and even farther from where he lived.

He saw that she'd understood.

"Knew a Ph.D. like you wouldn't be interested in your building manager," he said.

"Have I even seen you working here?"

"Couple times," he grinned. "But this uniform makes me invisible to people like you."

She sat in a chair across from the sofa.

"Do you mind?" she said. "Since you've already made yourself comfortable?"

He sat up to face her.

"Not going to ask what I'm doing here?" he said.

"Probably angry about my TPS rant," she shrugged. "And maybe I was a little harsh, but I've moved on. I have work, so you need to go."

He stood up.

"A little harsh?" he said. "I decide how people talk to me, and no one gets to talk to me that way."

He took a step toward her. She shifted in her chair.

"You humiliated me in front of the whole world."

"No one knew it was you," she laughed, stopping when she saw his reaction. "And I see now that I wasn't even talking to *you.* I was talking to somebody else."

"You were talking to someone with money and a good education. But if you can talk like you did to somebody like that, how would you have talked to me if you'd known I was only the building manager?"

Natalia wondered if she could get to the door before Mark could. He grinned again and took five or six steps to his left, positioning himself between her and the door.

"Where do you get this 'You wouldn't be interested in your building manager' crap from?" she said.

She thought she might do better by sounding angry rather than frightened.

"You're sure you had to lie? You never gave the truth a chance."

"The thing about not having a good education and working with your hands," he smiled, "is that your hands get strong."

Natalia shifted in her chair again.

"So, you're not married either? There's no Edith or Jimmy or Shirley, no in-laws in Duluth?"

"What did I see in you?" he said. "You're not that pretty, and you should be reading about what to do in bed instead of how to save the planet. Or don't you care about good sex?"

He took another step toward her.

"Is it just your job that gives you strong hands?" she said. "Or do you work out a lot?"

The only thing she could think to do was to keep talking.

"You know it's too late to save the planet, right? So, your Ph.D. and your research—all the stuff that makes you think you're better than someone like me—it's a waste of time."

Natalia realized that her attempt to sound angry rather than frightened had failed. She wondered if she ought to brush the tears off her cheeks but thought there was no point.

Mark took another step. He stood over her. He covered her mouth with his left hand. With his right hand he reached into his pocket. He pulled out a roll of Gorilla Tape. He took his left hand away from her mouth. He put its index finger to his lips. She had a moment to scream, but in her terror she could only obey. He tore a strip of Gorilla Tape from the roll. He placed the strip over her mouth and smoothed it down with his fingers.

"Remember what you kept saying when you were on TV?" he said. "Bet I heard 'Go fuck yourself, Mark' 50 times."

He laughed.

"I want to hear it 50 more times."

He wrapped his hands around her throat.

"Funny that I can't hear it now, though."

He tightened his grip slightly.

"But I can feel it in your vocal cords, so go ahead."

He tightened his grip a little more.

"I guess you didn't hear me: I said 50 times."

Natalia tried to say, "Go fuck yourself, Mark."

"Like you were doing on TV," he said. "Shouting—loud as you can."

Natalia tried to shout 50 times. Mark counted her attempts.

"Thank you," he smirked after the last try.

He hooked an index finger inside the V-neck collar of her dark T-shirt.

"We should have a permanent record of that," he said.

His hands gripped her collar on either side of the V. He tore the shirt open down to her waist.

"No bra," he said. "Tits that small you don't need one."

He reached into his shirt pocket. He pulled out a razor blade. He held it in front of her eyes. She closed them. She heard a sound she didn't recognize. She opened her eyes. He was wearing disposable plastic gloves. He held the razor blade in front of her eyes again and again she closed them. She felt a burning pain high up on her right arm, just below the sleeve of her T-shirt. She opened her eyes. She was bleeding.

"Good thing about your little tits," he said, "is they make a nice flat writing surface."

He dipped the finger of his plastic glove into her blood. She looked down. She watched him write across her chest. He stopped. It looked like *She sol*. He made a face.

"Too messy," he said.

He studied what he'd written.

"Don't believe in implants?" he said as he massaged the blood into her breasts.

"Move forward," he commanded.

She didn't understand.

"It's not complicated," he said roughly.

He gripped her shoulders and jerked her toward him. She shut her eyes and held her breath as the bitter stink of black coffee washed over her. She felt him yank her torn shirt down over her arms and hands. She realized that he was using it to tie her hands to the back of her chair.

He pulled away. She opened her eyes and watched him go into the kitchen.

"No paper towels?"

He laughed.

"Sorry," he said. "Forgot you can't talk."

She watched him go down the hall. He came back with a bath towel. He'd gotten one end of it wet. He used it to clean the blood from her breasts. He licked and sucked her right breast.

"You can admit it feels good," he laughed. "I'll never tell a soul."

He licked and sucked her left breast. He licked his lips.

"Clean now," he said.

He dried her with the rest of the towel. He dropped the towel on the floor. He took a Sharpie out of his shirt pocket.

"Red would be better," he scowled.

She watched him write with the black ink across her chest.

HE BEGAN TALKING again about why she'd been a poor choice for a girlfriend. He had more to say about her breasts. He had more to say about her alleged sexual inadequacy.

"Want me to start in on your other body parts?" he laughed.

She didn't hear most of his abuse. She was focused on reading.

He'd gotten as far as *She said go fuck yourself 50* at the moment when, abruptly, she became focused on something else: Wally, who had guessed the key code for her door—the year of her birth—and who now crept toward Mark from behind. He crept in silence thanks to his Anishinaabe moccasins. He had picked up the foot-long replica of Michelangelo's David, a souvenir of Natalia's undergraduate semester abroad in Italy, from the little table just inside the door. Natalia remembered telling Mark, exaggerating only slightly, that he was more beautiful than the

David. Wally raised the statue high above his head.

Mark sprawled unconscious and bleeding at Natalia's feet.

"Thanks," she said to Wally after he'd peeled the Gorilla Tape from her mouth. "But what are you doing here?"

"You didn't seem excited about the Sierras," he said while he untied her hands. "So, I wanted to tell you why it's a great idea."

Natalia thought she ought to call the police. Then she thought she ought to put on a shirt. Then she thought that now it would be hard to say no the Sierras.

"Can you wait for the police?" she said. "Even if it makes you late for your class?"

"It's okay," Wally said as he glanced at his watch. "I have 15 minutes."

Will our own madness save us from the machines?

LIGHTS OUT
Jo Perry

"Although the facility may run lights out ... that doesn't mean humans will be taken out of the equation completely. You will need some sort of staff to monitor the operation ... and troubleshoot any problems that arise. At least until the machines acquire enough intelligence to fix themselves.."

"Embrace the Darkness:Moving to the 'lights out warehouse,'"

FoodLogistics.com

PEOPLE SAY THEY sound like insects.

People are full of shit.

They—the Operatives—murmur as they skim the tracks embedded in the micro-engineered, nonabrasive surface—and if there's a goddamned insect that murmurs, I would have fucking heard about it.

They—the Operatives—are relentless, intelligent and precise.

And for the record, there are exactly eight sounds here besides the undying murmur they make—

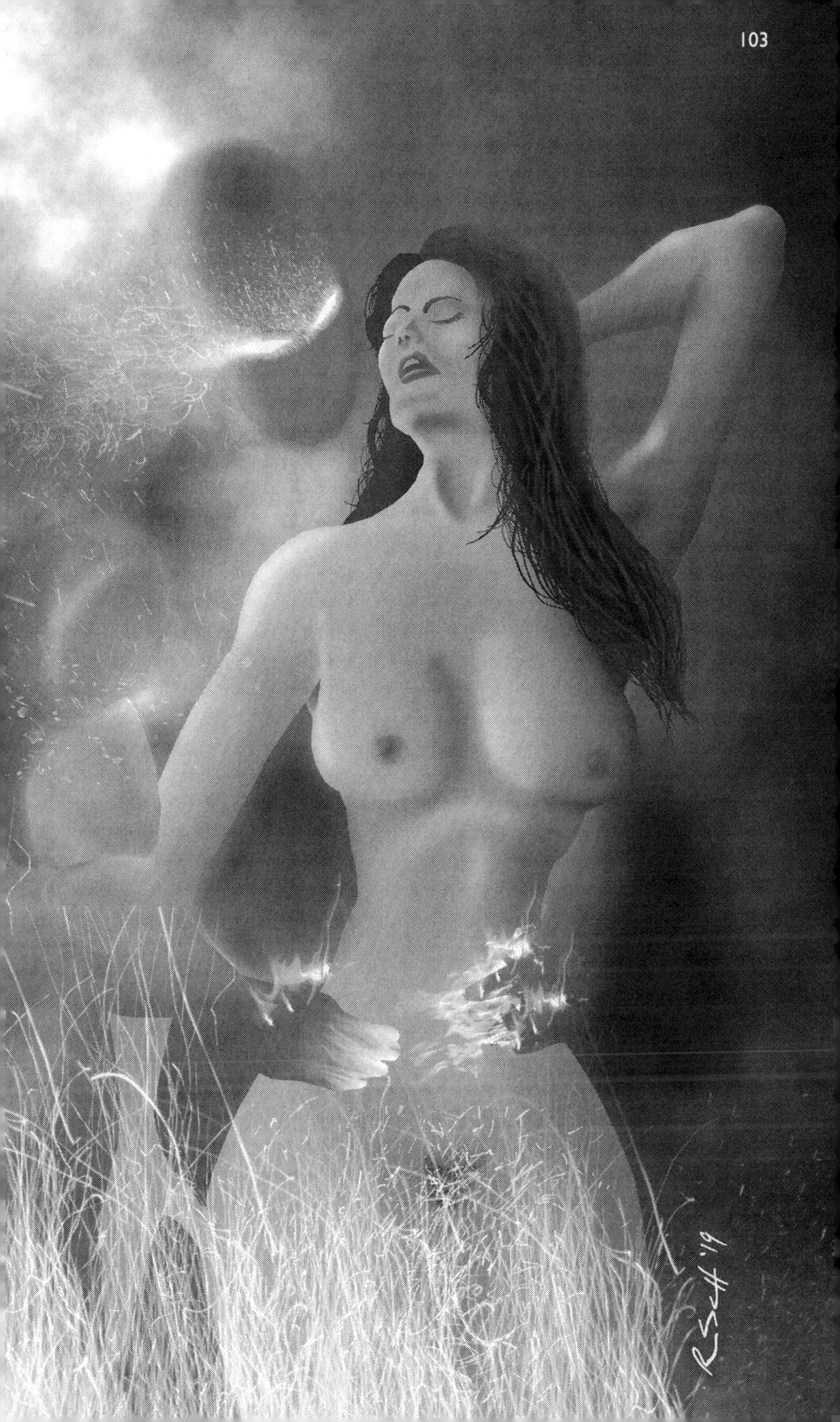

The rasp of metal against metal, the protests of accelerating and decelerating gears, the purr of the endless-energy illuminator here in the control chamber, the nutrition storage/waste elimination unit's vibrations, an intermittent crackling in my right ear from an ear wax problem, the creaks my fire-proof cold suit makes when I move, my respiration, and the noise of my voice inside my head.

More heat escapes from the head than anywhere else on the human body.

Viewed with thermal imaging, my skull would be spitting flames right now.

Do ants have voices?

What sound does a spider make weaving its web?

What explosion as the crystalline filaments stretch and fracture?

This facility is noise-proofed and completely Bio-Free—except for me, of course.

I imagine that cockroaches, iridescent beetles, and spiders click like tiny castanets and sing like miniature whales—don't ask me why—I just do.

Maybe because they operate in darkness.

Once—before my rehabilitation and training—I heard a recording of whales moaning and clicking. And behind their voices I heard a soundless roar.

I could add that the controls and the glowing keyboard click when I tap them—so those are two sounds or maybe one that I omitted—but who requested an auditory inventory anyway?

Not fucking anyone.

No talking.

No singing is permitted.

No music can mask the machinery's music.

But this period has been excellent.

I have been excellent.

I completed the Q12H inventory and system checks exactly on time.

And I am free from scheduled tasks for another quarter block except for the vigilance I must exercise at all times—without deviation or interruption.

Things are good.

I scanned and tested the autonomous guided material handling equipment, the execution systems, the automatic identification operations, the stacker cranes' optical hardware, and checked the drive and lift positions and cross beam detection.

Per-fucking-fecto.

The ventilation, cooling and ambient controls are precisely what they should be. The sub-zero chill beyond the triple-thick security and thermal-protective porthole instantly ices my breath on the dusky pane.

If you look into the dark all day, what do you see?

You see black holes eating dark matter.

What does dark matter eat?

High-density error-free operation is the goal, the necessity.

The supply chain demands perfect alignment within the racks, low-to-zero rejection rates while maximizing space.

It is my duty and mine alone to comply and to control.

People—there I go, using that word—which proves that no matter how thorough your rehabilitation, your training, and your emotional purging has been—or how regular your intake of sleep-murdering stimulants and psychosexual suppressive agents—certain thoughts will occasionally intrude upon your watchfulness.

But I know what to do.

When thoughts of bio-elements arrive, rely on your training.

Remember your duty.

Honor the supply chain.

Affirm your allegiance to the product.

And to the Operatives, of course.

The Operatives don't make mistakes.

I remember my mother telling me I was a "mistake."

As if the mode of production could define the product. What my mother didn't understand is that the product is everything.

The Operatives execute a continuous, complex, three-dimensional choreography in the freezing dark.

Make that four-dimensional.

The Operatives can speed up time or halt it at will.

They are infallible.

If anything were to go wrong—and it cannot—it certainly

wouldn't be because of them.

There is only one vulnerability—the Surveillance Engineer.

Wrong.

Not the Surveillance Engineer. Not if he or she is well-trained. The only hypothetical vulnerability is the tendency in all things toward disorder—toward violation and chaos.

Entropy is the fucking problem here—if there ever were to be a problem.

A fucking problem.

A problem fucking.

The Surveillance Engineer's task is to stop entropy, to ensure that nothing changes—especially now that fires have destroyed the eastern and southern compounds.

THE FIRES MEAN that capacity must double in the north and here in the west.

But entropy is a law of nature.

Which means that anything that could happen will happen—not now, but eventually.

For instance, my head really will explode.

Or I will kill someone—snuff out a bio-element that somehow breaches the compound's radioactively fortified exterior security apparatus and enters.

But that can't happen here where every motion is detected.

I would hear the heavy, insulated, knee-high boots hitting the warehouse floor from miles away.

Not if the bio-element were barefoot. Naked.

It could locate the surveillance, logistics and engineering control chamber moving like a shadow among the dark miles of three-hundred foot high product towers, could intuit the entrance codes, disable the three-hundred-and-sixty degree swiveling heat-sensing photo eye and after violating the icy threshold forcibly remove my fireproof cold suit.

Our mingled breathing would ice-over that goddamned porthole.

Jesus fucking Christ.

It is the naked intruder who set the fires.

I fucking know it.

If not the naked arsonist, then an encroaching, disordering force.

I feel it.

Feel her lammable vibration.

Her dangerous hum.

The top of my head is heating the inside my helmet. The hairs on my body stiffen against the absorbent interior of my suit.

Jesus.

The thing that could happen really is happening.

A warm body is displacing and rearranging the microscopically filtered, particulate-free, sterile, and hyper-refrigerated air molecules that fill the bio-free compound and which the fresh product requires.

My hands tremble as I set the system controls to Auto.

I disengage stiffly from the control chair, snap on my cyclorefractive goggles, and enter the emergency exit code into the keypad.

The vault-thick electronic door beeps, relinquishes me into the chilled blackness and shuts.

It takes a few seconds for the goggles to calibrate and then I see them—the Operatives—green-gleaming compressed darknesses transferring palletized product, thousands of them scuttling, executing perfect angles from product tower to product tower to steel pallet, murmuring to one another as they travel along the razor sharp tracks at the same speed—didn't I say so?—in no way making noises that resemble insects.

No.

The Operatives conspire in a metal language all their own.

They do not speak to me.

They sing to the naked arsonist, "Come here, now."

If anything were to go wrong—and it absolutely cannot—it certainly won't be because of the Operatives. They are infallible.

"What a complete load of shit that is."

The words are ice-bullets launched from somewhere near the top of the Sector 500 product tower.

I close my eyes until their sting subsides and the tiny white flares behind my eyelids fade.

"They're fucking robots. Robots moving shit. Shit moving shit." The voice laughs.

The voice is close now, right behind the stacker crane.

"The Operatives are state of the art, error-free autonomous, guided material-handling equipment. Bio-intrusions are not permitted among them. I'm afraid I must immediately remove you from the premises."

"You? A janitor to an army of fucking Roombas? You couldn't remove a turd from a goddamned sidewalk if I had a gun to your head. You're a Level D Security Associate in a crappy fulfillment warehouse in the middle of nowhere, you dumb fuck. And by the way, when was your last fuck? If there ever was a fuck."

"I am the Surveillance Engineer. I control and secure this compound," I say with frozen teeth. "I am this fucking compound."

My goggles unsnap and icy darkness surges over me.

I'm drowning.

"Grab my hand!"

"No."

"Hurry! Take it, you dumb shit. Here."

A bare hand grips my glove and I feel its heat as it leads me across the frictionless surface, then knocks me down, hard.

"Lose the suit. Let me warm you up. Come on, let's fuck."

I force the scorching hand away from my suit's removal zipper, gripping it hard enough to hear the bones break under the skin.

The arsonist releases a huff of air.

Something alive and slippery that is either a snake or a human tongue darts inside my right glove. The shock of contact lifts me off the floor and pitches me against a pallet heavy with product mummified in protective wrap.

My shoulder hurts. My hand stings inside the glove. The pallet rocks, then falls across the track, forcing the murmuring Operatives to concuss.

A confused hissing rises from the Operatives, then a throbbing, gut-twisting alarm convulses the dark warehouse.

"You have really fucked up now, asshole. And you broke my goddamned hand."

The maimed intruder—the arsonist—is correct.

The unbearably loud alarm signals a system-wide Class-A malfunction, a cascading error-sequence fatal to production integrity and a rupture in the supply chain—if I don't fix the problem immediately.

I crawl—slide really—feeling my way along the floor's glacial surface toward the control chamber. But the product towers are so high and close to one another, the product modules so massive, the tracks so laceratingly sharp, the whining from the gnashing gears inside the crippled Operatives so hysterical, and the alarm so confusing, I spin sickeningly in the opaque gloom.

"Over here." The arsonist mocks from inside a ceiling purification filter.

"No here, you dumb fuck." The arsonist is so close that the words dent my helmet and pierce my suit like arrows.

You. Dumb. Fuck.

The words detonate like lumps of phosphorus and eat through my cold suit to my skin.

Fuck.

I remove my electronic tactical weapon from my pouch, aim at the spot where I last heard the arsonist's voice and activate.

"Fuck you."

Thousands of screaming bio-lethal, incendiary titanium pellets swarm the compound, searching for and locating the naked intruder in a white flash of sparks.

Excellent.

Then one product tower ignites and then another. The massive structures writhe and collapse until the vast accretion of product becomes a heaving sea of flame.

Goddamn it. The supply chain is broken. Melted.

I release my helmet and yank it off, unzip my stiff, fireproof cold suit, wriggle my arms free and feel the leaden suit collapse around my boots.

I'm almost weightless.

The hairs on my head and on my body sizzle and smoke as I remove the boots, and my insulation socks.

The cold electrifies my fingertips, the tips of my toes, my nostrils, my ears, and chars my skin taut.

The murmuring of the Operatives—crushed and roasted beetles on their backs—has finally fucking stopped.

I smolder in the cremating product's blinding light.

"I'm ready," I shout to the arsonist. "To fuck."

"To fuck" rises above the glowing detritus and ricochets inside the roaring lunar silence of the warehouse.

And I wait for the naked arsonist's rough embrace.

Jo Perry is the author of the dark, comic mystery series, *Dead Is Better*, *Dead Is Best*, *Dead Is Good*, and *Dead Is Beautiful* from Fahrenheit Press. Her novella, *Everything Happens*, will be paired with a novella by Derek Farrell in a @69Crime a tete beche edition this winter, and her story, "A Discreet Personal Assistant," will appear in the *Crossing Borders* anthology spring, 2020. <authorjoperry.com> @JoPerryAuthor

© Jo Perry

"I think there's a spy among us. That
guy over there has a tan."

"The Creature from the Black Lagoon with The Seven Year Itch"

• Author and editor **James Reasoner** delves into his short novels for *Mike Shayne* written as **Brett Halliday**; his PIs Cody, Delaney, and Markham; his Redemption series, his Wind River series with **L.J. Washburn**; and much more.

• **Ward Smith** remembers Armed Services Editions—digests that are not digests.

• **Peter Enfantino** tackles *Startling Mystery Stories* No. 1–18, and a keen assessment of *Manhunt* 1954 July–Oct.

• **Vince Nowell, Sr.** dissects **Sol Cohen's** tactics to save *Amazing Stories*.

• **Richard Krauss** examines Charlie Chan's media empire, with special emphasis on Renown Publications' digest magazine.

• **Steve Carper** reports on the one, the only, Bronze Books and trailblazers **Luke Roberts** and **Jesse Lee Carter**.

• **Tom Brinkmann** exposes *The Creature from the Black Lagoon* with *The Seven Year Itch*.

• Fiction by **Robert Snashall** and **Joe Wehrle, Jr.**, with art by **Carolyn Cosgriff**.

• News updates from *Ellery Queen* and *F&SF*, to *Switchblade* and *EconoClash Review*, and everything in between—direct from their editors' lips

• Reviews of *Alfred Hitchcock's Mystery Magazine* May/June 2019 and *Broadswords & Blasters* No. 9.

• Over 100 digest magazine cover images, cartoons by **Bob Vojtko** and **Brian Buniak**, a poem by **Clark Dissmeyer**, first issue factoids, and more.

The Digest Enthusiast No. 10
160 pages $8.99 print, $2.99 digital.

Get your print copies from Bud's Art Books, DreamHaven Books, Mike Chomko Books, Barnes & Noble (online), eBay, or Amazon. *The Digest Enthusiast* is also available in digital format for Kindle and Magzter.

'Progress' is not immune to the grift and the double-cross.

WALKING OUT

Zakariah Johnson

"IT'S A GOOD deal, Rice Man. Think of your family."

"My ex-wife?" the prisoner snorted. "Fuck her."

I sighed. "Your kid then. He's got some kind of condition, right? Needs a lot of specialized care?"

"Shit, you know how many baby mamas I got rolling around this world? Try again, Hopper."

His prison bravado was par for the course, but his smirk turned to a scowl as he sneered at me. I had him. I knew the Rice Man's profile and knew how to manipulate it. "Yeah, that's something you care about, isn't it? The boy? You can help him, even if you're never walking out of here on your own two legs."

"And you neither, eh, 'Hopper'?"

I ignored the jibe. "What's it going to be, convict?"

He considered for a few moments. "How's it work?"

"Execution day we reroute your central nervous system to swap out your perceptions with the client. What you see, hear, feel—it's all swapped out with him. You still die, but your last moments will be a lot pleasanter."

"What's in it for the other guy? Why's he paying to swap with me? Just some rich prick looking for a thrill or cocktail brag?"

"You know what autoerotic asphyxiation is?"

"*Pfft*. Those freaks. Wait, you mean—"

I nodded. "Yeah. The electric chair's supposed to give the hottest ride there is. This guy wants a piece."

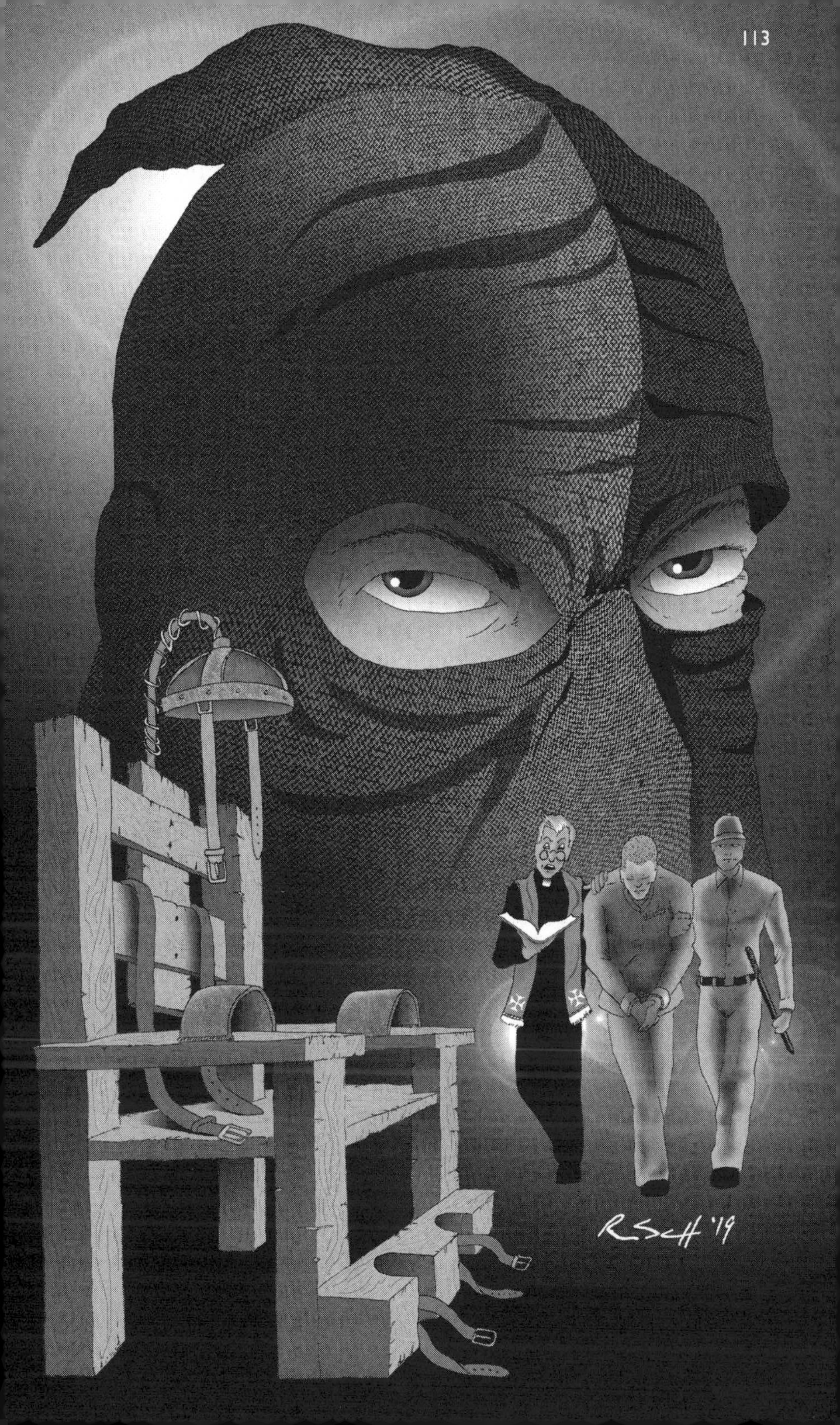
RSch '19

He shook his head. "And they call me sick. Tell you what, Hopper; I'm talking to Doc before I decide. Why don't you hop on over and get him for me?" His sneer was back in place, but I knew he was all in.

RICE MAN'S "HOPPER" jibes were in reference to my prosthetic legs. I didn't mind, they made me seven feet tall when I walked the prison halls in my open-backed culottes, and when I needed to cross the prison yard in two bounds to break up a fight or kick some ass, they unfolded like a pair of grasshopper legs to let me do it, lifting me up to a full ten feet in height where I could leap any distance or stare down the toughest con. Even without them, I was fiercer than I'd been when I started at the federal prison in upstate Maine, sixteen years earlier. I got shivved on my first shift as a guard, and, without antibiotics, the wound had cost me both my legs, at least my original ones. A hundred years of wasting antibiotics on chickens and cows had cost the world its greatest medical advance in history—antibiotics worked no more. These days a child could design a working artificial heart on a home 3-D printer, but most people would die of infection if they ever tried to install it. So, goodbye legs, hello "Hopper."

I KNOCKED AT Doc's office.

"Yeah?"

I stepped in and closed the door behind me.

"What'd the Rice Man say?" he asked.

"He's wavering. Claims he doesn't care about the money for his kid, but he does. Says he wants to talk to you first."

"What, the prisoners don't trust the guards?" He grinned. "What's the world coming to?"

I leaned against the door and crossed my arms. "We can't keep doing this."

Doc just shrugged. "Don't fret it. I got us covered with the admin. You think nobody else knows? Let me talk to the blue-veined SOB and I'll get back to you. Have him fake an injury and bring him to the clinic tomorrow."

I did. After his tête-à-tête with Doc, the Rice Man was in. For the right price, he'd do the swap.

RICE MAN (RIESE being his real name) was a black-haired, dark-eyed white man with skin already pale when he got sent to the federal death-row facility in upstate Maine seven years earlier. The first year, he formed a half-assed escape plan, which I personally thwarted, after which he was only let out of his cage into a small yard once a day for exercise and sunlight. But it's cold up here, and eventually he quit taking his legally mandated sunbreaks. After that, his skin faded to the pallor of a maggot, his black hair like the head where the tiny creatures have their mouths and eyes and whatever brain motivates them. The resemblance was uncanny. Sometimes the Rice Man reminded me of the live maggots the doctors had put on my infected stab wounds to try to save my leg. The beasts were supposed to eat away just the dead meat and save the rest, but my legs still got infected and had to be removed, along with my manhood. Being treated in Doc's filthy prison hospital probably hadn't helped.

Rice Man had earned his death sentence trafficking refugees from America's dying heartland towns onto ships bound for the floating work mills in the Spratly Island Free Enterprise Zone or other points in New Asia. Nothing unusual there, except Riese's smuggling ring only took migrants aboard long enough to harvest their pituitaries and livers for the underground medicinal *foie gras humain* market. They'd dump the bodies at sea and let whatever marine life was left take care of the evidence. Problem was, there were more bodies than the few remaining sharks could eat, and one day the Coasties caught up with them, following the trail of bobbing corpses. Rice Man was indeed not walking out of prison again. His legal appeals, however, could keep him alive for another decade or even the length of his natural lifespan, so it took a special deal like the body swap to get him to agree to drop them. Lucky for me, he still cared about his kid who never visited, the one whose medical expenses he'd claimed were his motivation all along.

"SO, HOW'S IT work, Hopper?" Riese asked me a few months later over the blow of the spring breeze. I'd used my seniority pull to get put on his guard detail, and he'd returned to visiting the miniature outside yard for "sunbreaks" so we could talk.

"Quiet down," I said out the side of my mouth. "I told you twenty times. We shave your hair for the electric chair, but then Doc implants a couple electrodes in your head. Under the bandages, nobody will notice beforehand, and afterward, your flesh will be too fried to notice."

"Doc takes care of the autopsy then? And nobody finds out?"

"That's right," I said, sneezing into the crook of my elbow.

"You got hay fever, Hopper?" Riese asked as I sneezed again. I ignored him. "How about cats, you allergic to cats? Any food allergies?"

"What do you care?" I asked.

He shrugged. "Just making conversation. What about infection?"

"From what, the implants? You'll be dead anyway. Don't worry."

"I mean for the guy paying for it? Won't he get a surgical infection, too?"

I paused to consider that. "Rumor is there's new antibiotics out there, if you can afford them."

"This guy's rich then? Like, rich-rich?"

"I suppose."

"You ever wonder what it'd be like to swap?" he asked.

"Wonder what it'd be like to have real legs again? Or a working dick?"

I looked up at the camera watching the yard and decided not to hit him. "Do some cardio," I said. "You'll live longer."

Rice Man just smirked as he huddled in his jacket and leaned against the fence, watching as the wind whipped the flag on the distant guard tower back and forth, back and forth to nowhere.

NEXT DAY, THE yard was busy. We have gun towers opposite each other on the northeast and southwest corners, but about 4 PM the sun dipped enough to put the southeast corner in shadow and the mess of prisoners there suddenly turned on the closest guards.

"Hopper—"

"On it!" I barked to my patrol partner, as my extra-long forelegs deployed and I bounded across the yard in seconds. Steadying on one foot, I used the metallic talons of the other to rip one, two, three, four cons in a row away from the two guards barely holding them off with their stun-sticks. The swarm turned on me, and I batted a couple away with ease before I felt one mount my back—someone must have boosted him. He got my arm and neck in a half-nelson, and then I felt the knife at my throat.

"Over the wall, Hopper!" he shouted in my ear. "You're taking me out of here! Go! Go!"

I spun round on my metal legs as more of the mob tried to climb me, the two guards I'd rescued retreating rather than helping me.

"Last chance, mother fu—*erk*!"

Bending my right leg entirely backward; first at the hip, then at the knee; I slammed the steel tip of my heel-talon into his neck, aiming for the base of his skull but striking him off-center. I caught his falling knife in my free hand as he went slack and his body flopped to the tarmac. The mob went suddenly silent as they stared up at me. Seconds later, a phalanx of guards plowed into them with stun-sticks swinging and the riot was over.

I crouched down to the wounded man. He was smiling, blood covering his teeth as he laughed at me, "You shoulda' gone over the wall with me, Hopper. You've been set up again . . . Rice Man's . . ." That was all he had time to say.

"HOW YOU DOING, Hopper?" the warden asked me in his office. After so many years, everybody called me that now, some as an insult, some out of respect, but most out of habit. I wondered how many of the new guards even knew my real name.

"I'm fine, sir. I don't need the time off."

"We can arrange it so you get full pay 'til the review's over," he said. "I owe you for stopping the escape. We both know it's my job if anybody gets out." Not just his job—as a former lifer like most wardens, an escape meant he was back in a cell himself.

"I'd rather not," I said, worrying about Rice Man's upcoming due date. "If it's all the same—"

"Damn it, Hopper," he said. "Thing is . . . the thing is, I can't keep you on anymore. Now that the prisoners have figured out you can scale the wall with those legs of yours, they'll be trying to ride you out every day. I gotta' let you go."

"You can't be serious? I'm four years away from my pension. How'm I supposed to eat?"

"It's money, then? That why you and Doc started playing mind games?" I didn't answer, so he went on. "You thought I didn't know? Your name badge, every doorknob, every toilet bowl, every button on every con's shirt in this shithole is a camera or a microphone. I know what you and Doc have been up to. Who do you think allowed it?"

"You get a cut then?"

"Of course I get a fucking cut, Hopper! Who you think runs this dump?" He sighed and sank into his chair, looking at me over his barren desk like a disappointed coach. I asked one more question.

"So, did the bug in my name badge tell you what that prisoner said before he died?"

The warden nodded.

"Do you know what he meant?"

He looked at me a long while, then picked up the remote off his desk and turned toward a big screen on the wall. He clicked the buttons until he got to the video he wanted. It was of Riese— Rice Man—and Doc talking soft and low in a room in the clinic. Talking about me. It turned out their tête-à-tête hadn't gone like Riese had told me.

"You get to the machine the day before," Rice Man whispered. "Turn down the juice enough to knock me out but not kill me. I swap with the client permanently."

"It can't be done, Riese," Doc said. "Your body's going in the incinerator. You're never walking out of here. The best I can do is get some money to your family."

"I don't need money, dumbass! I got MONEY!"

"How much?" Doc asked. Riese told him. Suddenly Doc was full of ideas on how Riese's "body" could be safely removed from the prison. For a price.

We watched the rest of the conversation to the end, then the warden erased it. "I owe you, Hopper, so I'll give you two more weeks on the job—your last day here will be the day of Riese's execution. How you deal with this is up to you, just know this: Riese's body isn't leaving these walls and Doc's not to know I bugged his clinic. And our client gets what he paid for—paid to you, to Doc, and to me."

I nodded. "That's more than fair."

RICE MAN WAS set to die at midnight. That afternoon, I shaved the condemned man's head and Doc inserted the implants.

"You'll have to remove the bandages at the back before you attach the helmet," Doc said. "Make sure the contacts are good. Otherwise, no transfer."

"Noted," I said.

"Hop to it, Hopper." Rice Man smirked.

Later on, the human maggot had his last meal—two Maine lobsters with corn on the cob, all boiled in a tub under fresh kelp. He told the priest to go fuck himself when he came in for last rites. Then he was ready.

"What's with the fucking hood, Hopper?" he asked me when I came to his cell wearing the old-style hangman's mask.

"Protocol," I said.

"You're seven feet tall, man. I mean, who the fuck else could you be?"

"Let's go, Riese."

We did the long walk, prisoners in their cells shouting through their tiny windows as the priest and a junior guard and I led Rice Man down to the death chamber. We passed an unmarked door where I knew Doc was hooking up the client I'd never met to a set of electrodes similar to Riese's.

"That where he's at?" Riese said.

"I'll take it from here, Father," I told the priest.

"What? I normally attend the—"

"Piss off, pedo," Riese told him. "Me and Hopper got a date with destiny."

We left the priest in the hall and entered the death chamber.

"Open the curtains," I told my junior. He did as told, moving to the far side of the room to reveal the thick one-way glass, behind which sat a few relatives of Riese's innumerable victims, along with a senator and the warden. The crowd of protesters outside the prison gates was tiny, both because we were way the hell up in northern Maine and because a guy with Riese's record made the worst possible poster boy for the anti-death-penalty crowd. All but the most fanatic learn to pick their battles.

"Up you go," I said, pulling Riese up into the big chair and then putting on the restraints. "Get behind your safety panel," I told the other hooded guard.

I moved around to the back of Riese's head as he expected me to and undid the bandages where Doc had inserted the electrodes. The skin around them was red and already starting to pustulate. I pulled down the modified helmet and stepped around to the side. Riese gave me a wink. He wasn't even breathing hard, not frightened at all.

I booted up the machine and moved toward the safety screen I'd stand behind to flip the switch.

I heard the warden's voice over the speaker, "Any last words?"

Riese started to respond, "I just want to say . . . hey, why I am still here?"

I spun the dials and rushed through the motions I had to make, pulling off my hood and snapping what looked like a pair of wireless headphones over the near-invisible electrodes protruding from my ears. I could no longer make out what Riese was shouting but wanted to be sure he didn't say more. I jammed the USB9 at the end of the wire running from Rice Man's helmet into the charging port on my left prosthetic and flipped the switch. My every nerve shrieked out in pain. My arms started flopping like trout on a riverbank, and my prosthetic legs twitched, then jumped on their own, slamming me into the ceiling before seizing up and shorting out. My eyeballs were burning and I felt one pop; then my teeth shattered under my clenching jaw and I felt myself falling. It felt like a dozen power drills were churning through my brains and the pain became too intense to retain consciousness, my last thoughts being that Doc and the warden had somehow fucked me good . . . .

"YOU OKAY?" SAID Doc, standing over me as I awoke in the hospital room. I looked around. It was a nice room. A private room. There were flowers on the dresser. I was no longer in the prison.

I looked down at my hands. They were dark and manicured, a platinum ring with a bright green emerald graced the left-hand pinky. Then I tried to wiggle my toes. I couldn't be sure it was working so I sat up.

"Pull the sheet back," I said. Doc pulled back the sheets and I saw my feet. My beautiful feet and toes; feet I could walk on, run on; toes I could stub and feel delicious pain through once more in a way I'd never truly felt with the bulky legs that had made me Hopper, "Grasshopper," the leaping prison-guard monster.

I wriggled my beautiful little toes and smiled at the doc. "I'm feeling fine, doc. How's Riese?"

"Riese is dead," he said, then he leaned in. "I got your body transferred out of the prison to a private facility. There was a slight infection but having access to the new antibiotics has its advantages."

I sat all the way up and turned to face him. He held up a mirror.

"Have a look, Mr. Vargas." I looked. I liked what I saw. I even liked the new name. It would cost me plenty to keep Doc and the warden happy, but now that I was "Mr. Vargas," money wouldn't be an issue.

See, what we didn't tell Riese was that the secret client— Vargas—hadn't really wanted to feel what it was like to die from 2,500 volts coursing through him, hadn't been some kind of sex addict looking for the ultimate orgasm at all. Instead, he'd wanted to know what it felt like to kill somebody, to kill legally by flipping the switch on the electric chair—he'd wanted to swap bodies with a guard, not a prisoner, just like the last two clients had. The guy had no link to Riese or any of Riese's victims whatsoever—he was just another rich asshole who wanted to know what it felt like to kill without consequence. I considered him no better than Riese, and I knew once he got a taste for killing that he'd be hooked on it—Doc and I had learned that much: they always got hooked. Best not to let them start.

The whole thing with Riese was a red herring for the post-execution investigation, something to explain why my comatose body would be found with a pair of electrodes sticking out of its ears. Doc had promised Riese that he'd be changing bodies with me (which the prisoner who climbed my back had somehow found out, forcing me to kill him). But that was just part of the sales pitch so Riese would let us wire him up. Doc would claim he knew nothing about it; ditto the warden. My browser history and the medical manuals found in my locker would suggest I'd had enough knowledge to do it myself. Nobody would be able to explain why the big prison guard had wanted to feel the charge ripping through him and had rewired his own brain with that of a prisoner (as it appeared I had.)

And the client? The one who'd wanted to know what it felt like to flip the switch? His mind would be routed through my comatose, legless, now-blinded and toothless body as long as it held out in the private hospital we'd transferred it to, the electrodes in his skull and in mine swapping our consciousnesses until one or the other of us died. And I intended to keep both our bodies healthy. I'd be free to walk the world — and indulge in other activities I'd thought lost me forever (Riese hadn't been wrong about my other missing body parts.)

I adjusted the small attachments that looked like old-fashioned hearing aids in my ears, then handed the mirror back to Doc, asking him the same question so many prisoners had asked me over the years:

"So, Doc, when am I walking out of here?"

Zakariah Johnson has been a mink rancher, halibut fisherman, archaeologist and the repeated target of hungry polar bears. His mystery & horror fiction + poetry appears in *Beat to a Pulp, Switchblade Magazine, Shotgun Honey, Sherlock Holmes Mystery Magazine,* and elsewhere. Zakariah lives in NH, where he's the cross-genre ("everything weird") editor for Folded Word press. Online @pteratorn.

Blood, Sweat, and Fears.

Stark House Press

JEFF VORZIMMER, EDITOR

The Best of Manhunt

978-1-944520-68-7 $21.95

Includes 39 of the original stories, a Foreword by Lawrence Block and Afterword by Barry N. Malzberg, as well as an introduction to the tortured history of the magazine by editor, Jeff Vorzimmer—with stories by David Goodis, Fredric Brown, Donald E. Westlake, Harlan Ellison, James M. Cain, Evan Hunter and many more. A bonanza of a book!

"This book comes most highly recommended to all readers of classic and contemporary crime fiction. In fact, if you read only one anthology of republished crime stories this year, it should be *The Best of Manhunt.*"
—Alan Cranis, Bookgasm

"...may be the greatest short story compilation... The stories are brutal and filled with final-page twists—or in other words: essential reading. Highest recommendation."
—Paperback Warrior

STARK HOUSE PRESS
1315 H Street, Eureka, CA 95501
707-498-3135 www.StarkHousePress.com
Available from your local bookstore, or direct from the publisher.

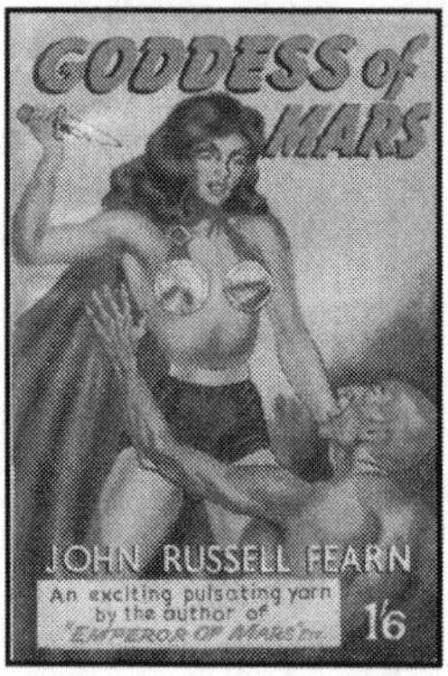
GODDESS of MARS
JOHN RUSSELL FEARN
An exciting pulsating yarn by the author of "EMPEROR OF MARS"
1/6

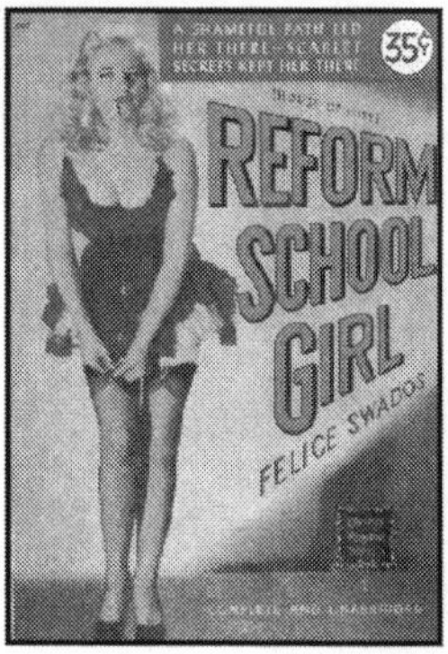
A SHAMEFUL PATH LED HER THERE—SCARLET SECRETS KEPT HER THERE!
35¢
REFORM SCHOOL GIRL
FELICE SWADOS
COMPLETE AND UNABRIDGED

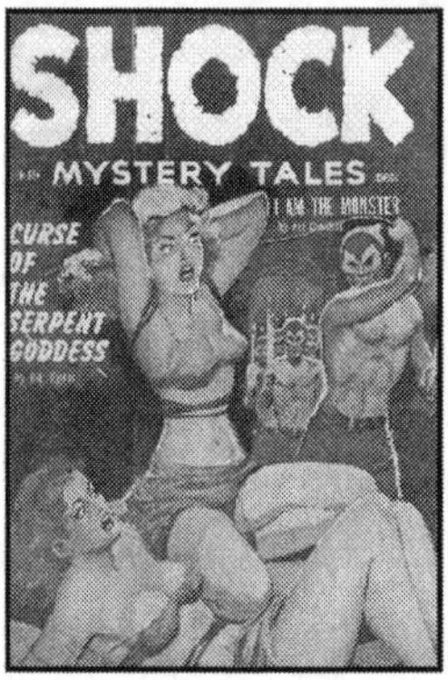
SHOCK
MYSTERY TALES
I AM THE MONSTER
CURSE OF THE SERPENT GODDESS

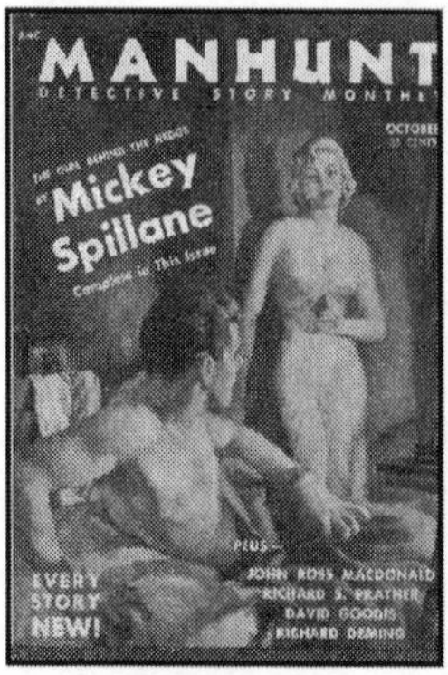
MANHUNT
DETECTIVE STORY MONTHLY
Mickey Spillane
Complete in This Issue
EVERY STORY NEW!
PLUS—
JOHN ROSS MACDONALD
RICHARD S. PRATHER
DAVID GOODIS
RICHARD DEMING

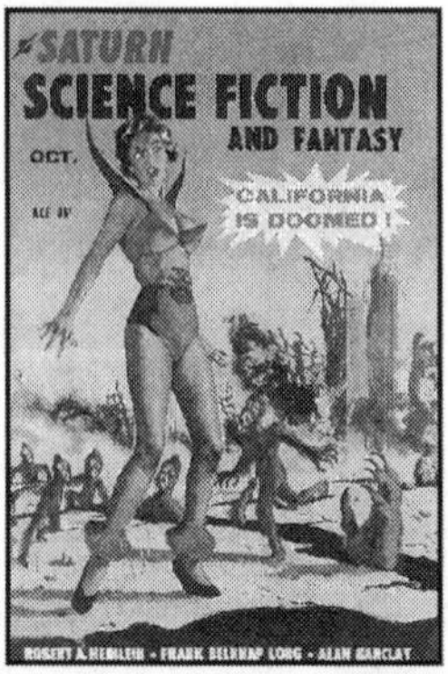
SATURN
SCIENCE FICTION AND FANTASY
OCT.
CALIFORNIA IS DOOMED!
ROBERT A. HEINLEIN • FRANK BELKNAP LONG • ALAN BARCLAY

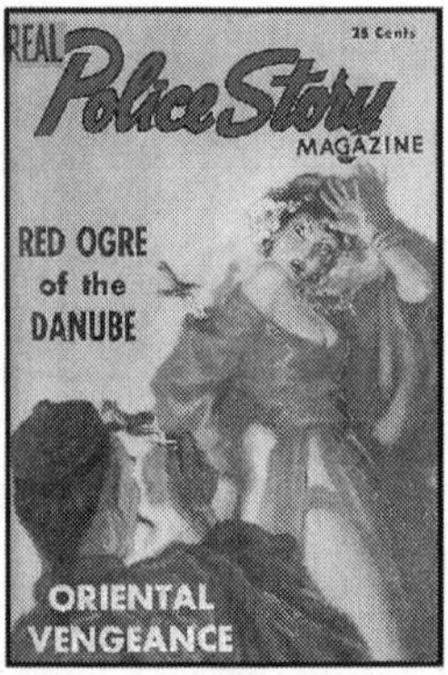
25 Cents
REAL Police Story MAGAZINE
RED OGRE of the DANUBE
ORIENTAL VENGEANCE

Contact

Get the latest news and announcements at <pulp-modern.blogspot> and <facebook.com/pulpmodern> Post feedback on Facebook or write to <pulpmodern@yahoo.com>

Links

C.W. Blackwood <facebook.com/cwalkerblackwell>
Deborah L. Davitt <edda-earth.com>
Nils Gilbertson <twitter.com/NilsGilbertson>
J.D. Graves <econoclash.com>
Zakariah Johnson <folded.wordpress.com>
Jo Perry <authorjoperry.com>
Ran Scott <Twitter.com/@RSPMystery>
Don Stoll <donstoll.naiwe.com>
Bob Vojtko <facebook.com/bob.vojtko.7>

Get a free ebook of *The Digest Enthusiast* book one on Magzter when you sign up for the Larque Press mailing list. More info at <LarquePress.com> For a daily dose of digest magazine news and history visit the Digest Magazines blog at <LarquePress.com>

Advertisers' Index

Made in the USA
San Bernardino, CA
06 November 2019